PART ONE

# CHAPTER ONE

# CADENZA TOWERS

SHOESTRING STOOD ON THE BALCONY AT the top floor of Cadenza Towers and looked out over the city. It was nearly evening and the audience would be arriving soon.

The moon wasn't up yet. What time did it rise? He should have checked. He had to have moonlight; if it was too dark no one would see him. His hands were sweaty and he wiped them on his white suit.

'May's not going to believe it. She's going to bust out of her bodice – she'll be that proud of me.' He was talking to himself but his friend KidGlovz heard.

'Isn't she proud already?' he asked.

Kid sat in the doorway with pages of music spread out before him. He wrote down some more notes.

'I want her to be *really* proud,' Shoestring replied. 'I want to be brilliant.'

'You can't help being brilliant with an act like you've got,' Kid said.

It was true. Shoestring's act was extraordinary. He felt for his rope and checked the knots one last time, resisting the temptation to undo them and start again. One end of the rope was fixed to the balcony railing, the other to the top of a tree that grew on the pavement beyond the garden wall. He'd secured both ends with a span loop, followed by two double half-hitches, then he'd finished off with an underhand stopper. He never used to worry about fancy knots when he was a street performer. In those days he wasn't far off the ground and he often needed to make a quick getaway, so he'd just use a simple bowline or a slipknot. His act was only a diversion then, something to make people look up while the other boys went about their work.

Shoestring thought how the boys would laugh if they saw him dressed as he was now. But they would stop laughing once they saw what he could do. He looked down at the white jacket. It was fine linen and the cut of it fitted him perfectly. It would catch the light and make him stand out against the night sky.

He gave the rope a tug. It had enough slack in it to let him swing out wide over the heads of the audience. He'd do that later in the act, after they'd got over the initial shock.

Shoestring leaned over the railing and looked down through the safety net into the garden where Grimwade and

Franko were arranging chairs. Eighty of them. Would eighty be enough?

'We need more chairs, Mr Grimwade,' he called out.

Grimwade used to be a bodyguard. Now he was a butler. He looked up and waved.

'No room, boy. Not without going into the flowerbeds, and your cousin here is already fretting over his delphiniums.'

Franko looked over the sea of chairs towards the beds that edged the garden.

'If any of my plants get stomped on I'm blaming you, Shoe,' he said.

Shoestring sighed. It was hard to believe Franko had once been a bandit. He turned to KidGlovz and spread his hands. 'Who cares about the delphiniums? This is the world premiere performance of the Troupe of Marvels. What does it matter if a few flowers get crushed underfoot?'

'It matters to Franko.' Kid crossed out two notes on the manuscript then turned the page. 'I'm not sure about the triplets at the end of bar sixty-three,' he muttered to no one in particular.

Shoestring looked back over the railing. The net annoyed him. He didn't need it and it would take the edge off his act. But Lovegrove had insisted.

'When I'm the boss of the troupe there'll be no net,' he promised himself.

Just then, Madame Lovegrove hurried into the room,

accompanied by Sylvie, the youngest member of the troupe. The little girl had a violin tucked under her arm.

Lovegrove was a tall woman. She was wearing a long evening dress and her best quaver earrings.

'Is it finished, Kid?' she asked.

'Just writing the last few bars. I did it in G-minor, Sylvie. Is that all right?'

'It's my favourite key.' Sylvie smiled and plucked a string.

'I'm almost as nervous as I was at Kid's first concert.' Lovegrove ran her fingers through KidGlovz's hair. 'He was tiny then. He was half your age, Sylvie.'

Kid squirmed but he couldn't help smiling.

'Yes, but now I'm eleven, Lovegrove. Not a baby anymore.'

'Of course, dear, of course.' She kissed him on the forehead, then produced a brush and began doing Sylvie's hair. 'Would you like it tied back? We don't want it getting caught up in the bow.'

Sylvie nodded. She took off her glasses and closed her eyes. She loved having her hair brushed.

'And how's the star?' Lovegrove asked. 'Excited?'

Shoestring stood at the doorway. 'The net, Lovegrove—' he began.

'It stays,' she replied. 'I won't budge on that. If you fell you could kill someone.'

'But it ruins the view. The audience will have to look up through it.'

'That will only add to
the mystery,' Lovegrove told
him. 'They will peer up and they
won't believe their eyes.'

There were voices below. People
were arriving.

Lovegrove tied Sylvie's hair with a
green ribbon. 'To match your eyes,' she
said. 'I'd better go. Good luck, everyone.'

Shoestring's heart began beating loudly.
He took a deep breath to steady himself and
looked beyond the wall. There was already a
queue and May was at the end of it. He waved but
she didn't see him. She was talking to Metropolis,
who sat on her shoulder. Shoestring wished she
hadn't brought the bird.

Franko was standing at the gate, greeting the guests.

'Hello, May. Hi, Metropolis.'

May kissed him on both cheeks. Metropolis glanced at him and began preening May's feather boa.

'Sulking again, is she?' Franko asked.

'She didn't want to come,' May told him. 'She thinks he's telling lies.'

'The boy can do it. I've seen him practising.'

*I'll believe it when I see it*, Metropolis thought, but she said nothing.

Franko took May and Metropolis inside and introduced them to Madame Lovegrove.

'Welcome to Cadenza Towers,' the tall lady said. 'Shoestring's told me all about you. He's saved you a place in the front row.'

Taking May's hand, Lovegrove led them to their seat and sat down beside them. The chair next to her was occupied by an enormous wolfhound.

'This is my dog, Hugo,' she said.

Metropolis looked sideways at the hound and changed shoulders, keeping her distance.

A net was strung above the garden like a false ceiling and through it Lovegrove and May could see Shoestring pacing up and down on a little balcony high above. He was wearing a white suit and he looked nervous.

'ARE YOU KIDS READY?' GRIMWADE POKED his head through the door. 'What a crowd! There must be a hundred people down there.'

*A hundred is nothing*, Shoestring thought. *Soon we'll be performing for thousands!* He looked down at May, hoping to catch her eye. She was talking to Lovegrove but Metropolis looked up and glared at him. Then she lowered her head, tucked a lock of hair behind May's ear and, flicking the feather boa over her shoulder, sat facing the front. 'We're on in five minutes,' Grimwade told them.

KidGlovz added the last note and handed the music to Sylvie, who cast her eyes over the page.

'Lovely,' she said. 'It ends with a top C.'

She put the music down and headed for the door.

'Don't you need to take it with you?' Shoestring asked.

'No. I'll remember it.'

The three of them followed Grimwade down the stairs. When they were in sight of the front door Shoestring turned to his friend.

'I want to be the best, Kid,' he said. 'I want to be famous like you were.'

'Fame isn't everything,' Kid replied, but Shoestring didn't hear. He ran down the last few stairs, leapt out the door and jumped onto the little stage that Grimwade and Franko had constructed on the front lawn.

'Ladies and gentlemen,' he announced. 'You are about

to witness an extraordinary event — the world premiere performance of the Troupe of Marvels for one night only.

'Tomorrow we go on tour. Our troupe is small but it will grow. Allow me to introduce…'

Shoestring watched Ace fan the cards. He did an undercut shuffle and passed them from one hand to the other. They danced in the air, and then with an elaborate flourish Ace fell to one knee before a lady in the front row.

'Pick a card, any card. Don't tell me what it is.'

The woman did as he asked. She glanced at the card and when she slipped it back in the pack Ace's hands moved so fast his fingers were a blur. He did a fanfaring shuffle that made the audience gasp, then he pocketed the pack and scratched his head.

'Now where could it be? Let me find it for you.'

The audience laughed when he pulled a card from beneath his collar.

'The three of clubs?' he asked. 'Surely not.'

He lifted a man's hat and found the four of spades. 'That's not it,' he cried. 'Then it must be...' – he pulled a card from May's feather boa – '...the Queen of Hearts!'

The woman clapped her hands in delight.

'How did you know?' she cried and May laughed heartily.

Ace gave a bow and the audience cheered. Shoestring took a deep breath. Now it was his turn. He spread his hands to quieten the applause.

'Ladies and gentlemen, next you will see a boy doing the impossible. That boy is me, Shoestring. I'm going to walk on air.' He turned and ran back inside the house.

Lovegrove took the stage. 'My student, Sylvie Quickfingers,

will accompany Shoestring with a composition by our own KidGlovz,' she said. 'It's called *Thin Air Sonata on a G-minor string.*'

Lovegrove gestured towards the balcony. Shoestring was standing on the edge of the railing. Grimwade provided a drumroll and without further ado Shoestring stepped forward. Metropolis raised her crest and let out a squawk. The audience gasped.

'It's true,' May breathed. 'I knew he could do it!'

Shoestring took a small bow as if that was just the beginning, then Sylvie played another air while Shoestring danced and leapt and somersaulted in time with the music. He did a couple of backflips and she picked up the tempo. Faster and faster she played and Shoestring vaulted in time, never missing a beat. The audience went wild. May clutched her hands to her chest and laughed with the sheer joy of it.

When the performance was over she hugged Shoestring tight. 'I'm so proud of you,' she cried. 'If you play your cards right you'll never have to steal again.'

May wished she could stay for the party afterwards but she and Metropolis had to go back to the Luck Palace. The customers would be arriving soon. She kissed Shoestring goodbye and he was quickly surrounded by an adoring crowd. Everyone wanted to talk to him.

'Incredible,' one woman said as she touched his invisible rope. 'Where did you get it?'

'It's a long story,' Shoestring told her. 'But basically, I stole it. It was at a place called Goat Mountain.'

'Where's that?' someone asked.

'Far from here.'

'Tell us about it,' the lady urged.

Shoestring was about to launch into the story when KidGlovz tapped him on the shoulder.

'Lovegrove says we should start packing. She wants us to have an early night so we can leave on tour first thing in the morning.'

'An early night! Who's she kidding?' Shoe cried. 'The night is young and it belongs to me!'

He turned to his admirers. He had a good mind to string his rope back up and perform all over again.

'Without the net this time,' he muttered, picturing himself high in the air, higher than before. He closed his eyes. The crowd below him was vast – ten times, no, a hundred times the size of this first audience.

Unbelievable!

14

He was so far above he couldn't make out the faces. The wind lifted his hair and his white suit glowed in the moonlight.

# CHAPTER TWO

# THE LUCK PALACE

'WASN'T HE BRILLIANT!' MAY SAID AS SHE and Metropolis headed down Viva Street. The macaw didn't answer.

'I thought he was spectacular,' she continued. 'I loved every minute of it, not just Shoe but the whole show.'

They reached a rundown-looking shop at the bottom of a two-storey building and Metropolis studied the sign on the wall as if she'd never seen it before.

E.E.GOLDFIEND
JEWELLER
AND PAWNBROKER
GOLD SILVER
BUY SELL LOAN

Mr Edwin Goldfiend looked up from the counter when they arrived. He'd been examining an unusual brooch – rubies in a gold setting – and trying to determine its value. It took a moment for his eyes to refocus.

'How did it go?' he asked, blinking.

'Marvellous, Mr Goldfiend,' May exclaimed. 'The boy's done us proud.'

She swept through to the back of the shop and up the stairs to the Luck Palace.

'Shoestring's come up trumps, eh May!' said Lobe, the doorman. 'What an act. If only my eyes were as good as my ears. I'd love to have seen it.'

May didn't need to tell Lobe about the show. He'd heard everything, even though Cadenza Towers was on the other side of the city. Lobe had extraordinary powers of hearing. That's why he was on the door. He could hear an ant change its mind at fifty paces. And he could hear trouble coming before it even began to brew.

'What did you think, Metropolis?' he asked,

'All right, I suppose,' the macaw answered. She was peeved that for once Shoestring had been telling the truth. The boy really could walk on air.

'She's not in the best of moods.' May gave Lobe a wink. She went past the gaming room and up the hall to her bedroom. She needed to get changed before the night's work began.

T HE THING I LIKE ABOUT MY CAGE IS ITS
gold-rimmed mirror. It's oval in shape and it frames
my face beautifully. The *Macoa macaurus fabulosa*, also
known as the Fabulous Macaw, is a magnificent bird and I'm
proud to admit I'm a member of that species!

'Metropolis, stop looking at yourself. We should be in the
gaming room by now.'

We had just arrived home and I was settling in, admiring
my splendid reflection, when May spoke. I turned my head,
not to look at May, Queen of Hearts, but to check out my
other profile. When you're as perfect as I am it's hard to
decide which side is best.

'What do you think, May? The left or the right?'

She ignored me. 'Shoestring was amazing tonight,' she
said. 'I want to give him a present, a little something to wish
him luck in his new career.'

I cocked my head, marvelling at my eyebrow feathers, which
are a unique feature of the Fabulous Macaw.

'What would you suggest?' May asked.

I dragged myself away from the mirror and looked around
our room. There were ornaments on the mantelpiece and
objects of value wherever you looked. Everything in the Luck
Palace had come from somewhere else. The furnishings had
once graced the great houses of Cadenza and the lamp next
to May's bed used to belong to a count who was so wealthy he
probably hadn't even noticed it was gone.

A lot of the stuff had been stolen by Shoestring. He was May's nephew, or she called him that. She'd actually won him in a card game when he was a baby. He was the best thief in town.

'Give him the lamp,' I told May.

She sucked on her pipe. 'Metropolis, don't be difficult. He needs something small.'

To tell you the truth I had no time for Shoestring. Before he came I had May to myself. Well, almost to myself. Ace was around; we'd put him on as a dealer as soon as we moved into the Luck Palace. When May decided to marry him I didn't object. We needed a skilled croupier and he was good with the cards.

Both May and Ace were pleased with the turn Shoestring's life had recently taken. He was out of the gang and heading in a new direction. Ace had gone with him to keep an eye on him.

'Give him your brooch.' I said it to annoy her.

It was the brooch that held her turban in place, a piece that Mr Goldfiend in the hock shop downstairs could easily have sold a hundred times over, but May had taken a shine to it. She'd acquired it back in the old days before she even owned the Luck Palace. Mr Goldfiend said it had once belonged to a queen. When she put it on she got her name – May, Queen of Hearts. Ace called her that and it stuck. The brooch was special to her.

'I've got a better idea,' she said with a wink.

To My
Darling Boy.
For the
Future!
love
May

May was a big woman but her hands were small and quick as lightning. Her mind was quick, too. I should have slammed the door of my cage and locked it from the inside but she was too fast for me. In a flash she snatched my mirror and put it on her dressing table, where she polished it with a silk handkerchief.

'Small enough to slip into his pocket,' she said. 'Just the thing!'

Her laughter echoed in the hallway and it must have reached the card parlour because soon everyone was poking their heads through the door to see what the joke was about: Lobe, Ruby the waitress, the kitchen staff, and half a dozen boys from the gang. May's laughter must have carried all the way downstairs to the shop because even Mr Goldfiend appeared, his eyes watering behind his wire-rimmed glasses.

May sent one of her boys off to deliver the mirror. I wasn't amused. My feathers were ruffled and my beak was out of joint.

The night had got off to a bad start.

'COME ON, METROPOLIS. I CAN'T BE WAITING all night,' May said.

'I'm not coming.' Metropolis closed the door of her cage and turned the key.

May went to the gaming room without her. She looked out over the tables. The place was already crowded. Ruby was rushing back and forth to the kitchen, trying to keep up with the orders. The Ditto Twins were doing a number on top of the piano but there was so much noise she could barely hear the clicking of their tap shoes. The barman looked harassed. He signalled to one of the card-sharps for help but he was ignored.

An argument broke out at a table near the back. 'You cheated, you dirty rat. I'm going to punch your lights out!'

May glided across the room towards the offenders.

'Gentlemen, mind your manners,' she said as she picked two men up by the scruffs of their necks. 'This is a respectable establishment.'

'Respectable, my armpit,' one of them yelled, then he fell silent as May carried him towards the door, which Lobe held open in readiness. She paused briefly to taste a piece of cake that Ruby offered from the end of a knife.

'Cookie wants to know if she was too heavy-handed with the cherry brandy,' Ruby said. 'What do you think?'

'Delicious!' May declared, then she threw both men out the door.

W HEN I'M IN A GOOD MOOD I THINK OF THE
Luck Palace as a great wooden galleon, a pirate ship
with May as its captain. I perch on her shoulder as she moves
across the deck. We are sailing the open ocean and the stakes
are high. If she joins a game I make it my business to study
the hands of her opponents, especially newcomers who have
no idea of my abilities. I conceal myself in one of the potted
palms that have been positioned behind the players, or I flap
up to the chandelier and hang there, sometimes upside down,
which can cause even the best card player to lose concentration.
Then I hop back to May's shoulder and whisper in her ear. At
such times she will smile to herself before raising her bet,
challenging the company to do likewise. She always wins.

But that night I was not in a good mood. So I stayed in
my cage and put my head under my wing, trying to block out
the noise from the gaming room — the hum of conversation,
occasional bursts of laughter and the endless rattling of dice.
I didn't even say goodnight to myself. How could I, when my
mirror was gone?

# CHAPTER THREE

# THE TOWER OF DIAMONDS

'YOU CAN FEEL IT BUT YOU CAN'T SEE IT.' Shoestring passed his rope around the crowd of admirers and looked across the garden. Franko had stacked the chairs against the wall and people were dancing on the lawn. KidGlovz had done some packing and returned to join the party. He was playing his accordion. When Shoe caught his eye Kid pulled the bellows out wide and pretended to stagger under the weight of the instrument. Shoestring laughed. The show was over but many guests had stayed on to enjoy the evening. Grimwade and Franko were serving refreshments.

Sylvie had the top room at Cadenza Towers, the room with the balcony. She leaned over the railing and called down.

'Lovegrove says you boys have to come in. We're leaving at first light.'

She left the balcony and went back into her room. Lovegrove was laying out her things on the bed. Sylvie began folding them up and putting them into a little suitcase. Hugo watched, thumping his tail on the floor.

'You played beautifully tonight, my dear.'

'It's your good teaching, Lovegrove.'

'Now, what else do we need? We don't want to take too much.'

Sylvie was a collector. She was only five but she'd gathered many things in her short life. She had albums full of stamps and special labelled boxes full of shells, feathers and buttons. Her shelves were stacked with sheet music, including all KidGlovz's compositions, and the diaries in which she collected her thoughts were lined up in rows with the dates printed neatly on the spines.

Sylvie looked around the room.

'I've been happy here,' the little girl said. 'But I've been sad as well.'

'I know, Sylvie.'

Lovegrove sat down on the bed. She remembered the day she had arrived at Cadenza Towers and found Sylvie locked in this very room. She was a poor frightened three-year-old and she clung to the clasps on her belt as if they were the only things holding her together.

It was an unusual belt and she was still wearing it. Instead of a buckle it had two scroll-shaped clasps that fitted one into the other, and the fabric was embroidered with fiddleheads, each frond stitched in green thread. The belt was much too small for her now. She had it tied together with string because the clasps wouldn't do up anymore.

'You've really grown too big for that belt, Sylvie,' Lovegrove said.

'I'd never leave it behind. It's the only thing…'

'I know. Maybe I could put a piece in it for you so it will fit.'

'Thank you, Lovegrove.' Sylvie took off the belt, then put on her pyjamas and continued packing. She put two blank diaries in her suitcase, along with her favourite book and an empty box in which she could collect new treasures.

'Sleep well, little Sylvie.' Lovegrove kissed her goodnight and left the room with Hugo.

'WHAT A SHOW!' SHOESTRING SAT UP IN BED and looked at himself in the mirror. He'd tied it to a piece of string so he could wear it around his neck like a pendant. He thought he looked different somehow. What was it about him? He couldn't quite put his finger on it. He looked older and stronger. He breathed on the mirror, fogging it up, then rubbed it on his shirt and checked again. Yes, that's what it was – he looked older. He looked grown up.

'Where did you get that?' Kid asked, a hint of suspicion in his voice. 'You didn't steal it, did you?'

'Course not. May gave it to me. It's a present. It's to bring me luck.'

Shoe pressed the mirror to his chest. 'Thank you, May,' he whispered. She always gave him exactly what he needed. She'd done it since he was a baby and he loved her with all his heart. He'd made her proud tonight but that was nothing compared with what he'd do in the future. She wouldn't believe the heights he would reach.

Shoestring smiled. 'Tonight was wonderful, Kid.'

KidGlovz nodded. 'I liked it better than any of my concerts. Have you packed your things?'

'All I need is this mirror, my rope and a change of clothes. Goodnight, Kid.'

Shoestring fell asleep almost immediately. There was a full moon outside his window and he saw the same moon in his dream. He and Kid were walking in the mountains when they came across a boulder on the path ahead. It appeared to be rocking.

'There must be something under it,' Kid said, and he put his hand on Shoestring's arm, holding him back.

'Impossible,' Shoe said. 'What could move a big boulder like that?'

As he stepped towards it a cloud covered the moon. The sky darkened and the air grew suddenly cold.

'Look out!' he screamed. 'The gloves!'

'Shoe, wake up! You're dreaming!'

KidGlovz lit the bedside lamp.

'No, no, no!' Shoestring cried. He sat up and stared straight ahead. Then he shook his head and blinked.

'Are you all right?' KidGlovz put his arm around the older boy's shoulders. The door opened and Lovegrove looked in. She was wearing her dressing gown.

'Did someone call out?'

'Shoe had a dream,' Kid said.

'It was a nightmare.' Shoestring realised he was shaking.

'Would a hot drink help?' Lovegrove asked. 'Perhaps I could tell you a story?'

Shoestring shook his head. He was too old for that sort of thing. 'It's nothing, Lovegrove, just a silly dream. But thank you.'

When Lovegrove closed the door he looked in the mirror. The boy who stared back was young and scared.

'You called out about the gloves,' Kid said.

'They were coming for me. They looked like they were stitched together with horsehair. They were reaching for my throat.'

Kid frowned. Why would Shoe dream of the gloves? They were long gone. They were dead and buried.

'Go back to sleep, Shoe,' he said. 'We've got an early start tomorrow.' He blew out the lamp but neither of them slept. Kid tossed and turned and Shoestring lay on his back staring at the ceiling. His heart was hammering in his chest. To steady himself he thought of the gloves – not the terrible gloves in his dream, but the real gloves, the ones Kid had worn when he was the best piano player in the world. Shoestring took a deep breath and felt his fingers tingle the way they used to when he was a thief. A short time later he slipped out of bed.

Kid sat up. 'What are you doing?'

'I've got to find out what that dream means. I'm going to the Luck Palace.'

KidGlovz relit the lamp. 'But it's the middle of the night. Are you sure you're properly awake?'

'May will tell me. She'll get Metropolis to read the cards.' Shoestring pulled on his clothes. 'I won't be long. I'll be back by dawn.'

'We have to *leave* at dawn.' Kid looked at his friend with concern. Shoestring's eyes were wide open and he looked strangely excited.

'I think I'd better come with you.'

'No need. I can go by myself.'

'I'll come,' Kid said.

The two boys hurried across the city. Shoestring had told KidGlovz all about the Luck Palace but he'd never been there before. They left the leafy avenues of Upper Cadenza and once they passed Royal Parade they entered a part of the town where the streets were dark and narrow. Shoestring turned a corner and pointed to a shabby two-storey building at the end of a lane.

'This is it,' he said.

There was a jewellery shop on the ground floor and Kid was surprised to see a light on inside.

'Open at this hour?' he asked.

'Goldfiend does most of his business after dark.' Shoestring led Kid inside. Two men were leaning on the counter and Mr Goldfiend was deep in conversation with them.

'I'm sorry, we're not interested in diamonds,' he said. 'May won't touch them.'

'But these are best quality—' one of the men began.

'Have you got anything else?' Mr Goldfiend gave Shoe a nod as the boys went past.

'Three watches, two wedding rings and this.'

Kid saw a glint of silver as a bracelet changed hands over the counter.

'*To my darling P with love,*' Mr Goldfiend muttered. 'I can file off this inscription. Shall we say … three hundred for the lot?'

'Done!'

Kid followed Shoestring through to the back of the shop and up a narrow set of stairs. A man stood at the top.

'Congratulations, Shoe. I heard you brought the house down with that rope trick of yours!'

Shoestring introduced the doorman. 'This is Lobe.'

'Where's your accordion, boy?' Lobe asked. 'My word, you can play.'

A puzzled look passed over Kid's face. He hadn't seen the man at the performance and he felt sure he would have remembered him because the fellow was tall and thin and had the longest earlobes he'd ever seen. Lobe noticed the boy staring.

'I was an elephant in a past life.' He pulled one ear and grinned.

When he opened the door KidGlovz gasped. The inside of the Luck Palace was quite different from the outside. Gaslights and chandeliers lit up a lavish interior. The walls were hung with paintings in gilt frames and dozens of people sat at polished tables. Some were intent on card games but others were eating and talking. The windows were draped with heavy velvet curtains and the carpet was a deep red. If it wasn't for all the tables the place would have reminded Kid of the Cadenza State Theatre, where he used to perform. There was even a piano in the centre of the room.

'Shoestring,' cried May. 'What are you doing here? Shouldn't you boys be asleep? You're leaving in the morning.'

'I need Metropolis to read the cards.'

'But darling, she's in bed.'

A waitress swept past with a tray piled high with glasses. 'There's trouble in the back room, May,' she said.

'Shoestring, can you wait?' May hurried out the door and Shoe led KidGlovz through the tables to a quiet corner on the far side of the room where they sat on a couch in the shade of a potted palm. There was a set of nested tables in front of them and a fancy clock hung on the wall above their heads. Two girls, decked out in matching butterfly outfits, began dancing on the piano. *That would never happen at the Cadenza State Theatre*, Kid thought.

'They're Lobe's daughters,' Shoestring told him.

Kid watched them for a while. The girls were younger than he was. They had wings on their costumes and each held a butterfly net. He wondered how they could stay up so late. He yawned and looked at the clock. It was ten past two. He wished he'd told Lovegrove where they were going. If she woke up and found them missing she would worry.

He must have dropped off to sleep because he heard the clock chime and when he looked again it was three o'clock. The room was more crowded and May was sitting next to Shoestring on the couch.

'...and then the gloves came at me, May. I think it means something.'

She slipped her hand into the bodice of her dress and pulled out a pack of cards.

'Where's Lobe?' she asked, looking across the room. 'Ah, here he comes.'

Lobe was walking through the crowd with a disgruntled Metropolis perched on his shoulder. He placed her on the back of the couch and her eyelids drooped.

'Sorry to disturb you, old girl,' May said.

The macaw opened her eyes. 'I'm not old.'

'Well, you're no spring chicken, and neither am I.'

May began shuffling the cards.

KidGlovz looked at the bird. Shoestring had told him that she spoke but he hadn't believed it. He reached out to touch her.

'Careful, sweetheart. She pecks.' May pulled out a table and laid some cards face down.

'Where's the Queen?' somebody yelled. 'May, come over here!'

'Pick a card, love,' May said as she stood up. 'I won't be a minute.'

She headed to one of the tables.

Shoestring turned over a card. It had a picture of a tower being struck by lightning. A dragon was curled around its base and the stones of the tower looked like diamonds or exploding glass. Metropolis raised her crest in alarm.

'Calamity!' she squawked.

35

'Calamity. Catastrophe. Disaster!'

At that exact moment a shrill whistle pierced the air of the gaming room. *Too-wit too-wooo.* Everyone looked towards Lobe. He was standing at the door and he whistled again. *Too-wit too-wooo.*

'What sort of bird was that?' someone muttered in the silence that followed.

'A jailbird,' May replied. 'Everybody out!'

There was chaos as the room was cleared. A screen slid across the front of the bar and Kid watched while the cards, the customers and the tables were swept away.

'What's going on?' he asked.

Shoestring leapt to his feet and suddenly the two girls were beside Kid.

'Quick!' they said, each taking one of his hands. 'Out the back way.'

They pulled him towards a door he hadn't noticed was there. Shoestring was already running ahead of them. Two seconds later Kid looked over his shoulder and saw that the room was empty except for May, or a woman who looked like her. She was wearing a dressing gown and slippers and instead of a turban she had feathery hair that was piled high on her head.

'Ruby, the teapot and cups,' Kid heard her say as the Dittos pulled him outside onto a set of stairs that ran down the back of the building.

'Hurry,' they whispered.

# CHAPTER FOUR

# TROUPE
# OF MARVELS

TAP-TAP-TAPPITY-TAP. THE DITTOS' SHOES rang out on the cobblestones in the lane behind the Luck Palace. Shoestring turned the corner into Viva Street and the girls followed, their wings bouncing up and down. Kid ran along behind.

'I'm Daisy,' one of the girls called over her shoulder.

'And I'm Violet,' her sister said.

'My name's KidGlovz.'

'We know. We've read about you.' The girls flashed him identical smiles as they ran.

They knew which way Shoestring would go – he'd pass the bakery then turn left into the alley that led to Wobby's Lane, where Ruby's sister lived. If her light was on, they'd go in and wait there. If there was no light they would sit on her back stairs and maybe work out the steps to a new dance until it was safe to return. The raids at the Luck Palace never lasted long. But Shoestring didn't turn left into the alley. Instead, he kept going along Viva Street.

Calamity. Catastrophe. Disaster. Metropolis would say that, he thought as he ran. Shoestring saw the card in his mind – the flash of the lightning bolt, the broken tower, and all the bright tumbling stones.

*I'm not scared*, he told himself as he turned into Royal Parade. *My life is changing. Things get shaken up.* He pictured the dragon and felt a surge of energy. He sprinted to the end of the street then hid in a doorway and waited for the others to catch up.

'This is not the way,' the Dittos cried. 'Where are you going?'

'Kid and I have to go back to Cadenza Towers. We're leaving at dawn.'

There was already a faint glow over the roofs of the buildings. The sun would be up soon.

'Leaving for where?' Daisy asked.

'We're going on tour.'

Shoestring squatted in the doorway and Daisy and Violet sat down on either side of him, waiting for him to explain. By the time KidGlovz caught up with them Daisy had decided she would like to go on tour as well. Violet was of the same mind. The thought of travelling the country with the Troupe of Marvels and performing for a different audience each night was exciting.

'They want to come with us,' Shoe told Kid. 'They're contortionists and they can sing and dance. What do you think? Should we let them?'

Kid was almost out of breath. 'Shoe, that card...' he began. 'Maybe we shouldn't go on tour.'

Shoestring waved him away. 'You girls are welcome to come,' he said. 'We need more acts.'

Just then they heard running footsteps.

'Daisy. Violet. Where do you think you're going!' Lobe called out.

'Shoestring has asked us to join his troupe,' Violet said.

'Can we, Dad? Can we join?' her sister asked.

'I know what he said,' Lobe panted. 'I'm not letting you girls go off by yourselves.'

'Then come with us,' Shoestring suggested. 'We could use your ears, Lobe. We could work up an act around them.'

This idea delighted the girls.

'Brilliant!' they chimed.

Lobe was doubtful. He tugged one ear and his long face seemed to grow longer.

'What about May?' he asked.

'She's had other doormen before you,' Shoestring said. 'She'll find someone to take your place.'

'Please can we, Dad? Please?'

Over the years Lobe had learned to filter out most sounds he didn't want to hear. Without this skill he would get no rest.

But one sound he couldn't filter out no matter how hard he tried was the sound of his daughters' pleading, particularly when he had one in each ear as he did now. It amazed him that these two girls, who had the sweetest voices in the world – voices that could melt the hardest of hearts – could also make a frequency that not only set his teeth on edge but could threaten the very fabric of his being.

'All right,' he said. 'Let's go.'

IT WAS LIGHT BY THE TIME THE FIVE OF them arrived at Cadenza Towers. A wagon was parked on the street outside the wall and Grimwade was stacking pots and pans in the back of it. Ace came through the gate with his arms full of blankets.

'Coming with us, Lobe?' he asked.

The doorman spread his hands. 'The girls have made up their mind. You know how it is.'

Sylvie was already sitting on the wagon seat with her violin case under her feet.

'What's your name, little girl?' the Dittos asked.

'Sylvie Quickfingers.'

'I'm Violet and she's Daisy. You can tell us apart by our earrings.'

They showed her their ears, which were small and delicate

and nothing like their father's. Daisy was wearing a tiny white flower and her sister's earring was the shape of a violet.

'We're double jointed,' the twins explained, and Violet demonstrated by bending back and putting her head behind her knees.

Sylvie was normally a serious child but she laughed with surprise.

'Sit up here, next to me,' she told the girls.

They sprang up onto the wagon and sat on either side of her.

Ace introduced Lobe to Lovegrove and soon they were ready to go.

'All aboard!' Grimwade yelled. 'Boys, get your things.'

Hugo barked with excitement when Lovegrove took her place on the front of the wagon next to the girls. Grimwade climbed into the driver's seat and everyone else piled in the back. They were all laughing except for KidGlovz, who looked at Shoe and frowned. He felt uneasy about the journey ahead.

'What about that dream?' he asked.

Shoestring shrugged. 'It was nothing. We all have bad dreams now and then. Give us a tune, Kid. Something upbeat.'

Kid got out his accordion and although he was worried and had hardly slept the night before, it didn't show in his playing. Sylvie joined him on the fiddle and the Dittos leapt to their feet and danced as the wagon pulled out onto the street.

# CHAPTER FIVE

# CALAMITY, CATASTROPHE, DISASTER

METROPOLIS PERCHED ON THE BEDHEAD above May, who was snoring soundly. She couldn't get the card out of her mind. When she closed her eyes she saw the tower shattering into a million pieces. It was one of the worst cards in the pack.

*Calamity*, she thought. The word frightened her as much as the card. 'Still, I suppose he had it coming,' she muttered. 'Pride before a fall and all that…'

She looked at the sleeping May and sighed. 'Poor May. She'd die if anything happened to the boy.'

Metropolis flapped across the room and landed on the mantelpiece next to Shoestring's photo. There he was as a cheeky three-year-old. 'He was full of himself even then,' she muttered. Shoe had just stepped off his tightrope. May was holding his hand. She looked young and glamorous then, Metropolis thought. And so did the bird on her shoulder.

In the photo, Metropolis was posing; she stood on one leg and had a long-stemmed cigarette holder in her claws.

The wall behind the mantelpiece was covered with newspaper clippings. More than once May had made front-page news in the *Cadenza Times*. Metropolis read the headlines: MAY, QUEEN OF HEARTS – GANG LEADER WITH THE HEART OF GOLD and CRIME BOSS SAYS KINDNESS RULES.

Metropolis hopped past May's ornaments – a china dog, three brass monkeys and a hinged scallop shell with a pearl the size of a marble nestled inside it. She passed a mug shot of Ace and one of Franko and then she reached May and Ace's wedding picture. May's brooch caught the light and her smile was as wide as the world. The wedding party stood behind the couple and included the entire underworld of Cadenza city. Everyone was dressed to kill. Metropolis sighed and hopped back to Shoestring's picture. *Maybe I should warn him not to go on tour*, she thought. *For May's sake.*

She looked at Shoestring in the photo and remembered what a pest he'd been when he was small. He was still a pest, causing her to consider going out in the cold and dark. She looked towards the window. It was very late and she needed her beauty sleep.

*I'll think about it in the morning*, she decided, as she flew back to the bedhead.

IF METROPOLIS HADN'T DOZED OFF SHE might have seen something move outside the window. If she'd opened one eye she'd have noticed a hand parting the curtains, a gloved hand. A *thief,* she might have thought, *a thief in dark clothes and white gloves.* She might have watched the gloves moving about the room, picking things up and examining them. She would have seen them pause at the mantelpiece, tracing a finger along the top of the frame that held May and Shoestring's photo before suddenly plucking it from its place.

But Metropolis saw nothing because she was sound asleep. She didn't sleep for long though. She woke early and was annoyed with Shoestring all over again. She usually slept a good ten hours and rose well after midday, by which time May was busying herself in the card parlour preparing for the night ahead. But that morning was different; it was still dark and May hadn't moved.

'That boy's upset my natural nocturnal rhythm,' Metropolis muttered as she yawned and stretched her wings. She looked about the room. She had a vague sense that something important was missing, and when her eye rested on the cage she remembered what it was. May had given away her mirror. It was unforgivable. Worse than unforgivable; it was an outrage.

**T**HEY SAY THE DARKEST HOUR IS BEFORE dawn but I don't agree. If you've hardly had a wink of sleep even the dawn is dark. Brooding – that's what I was doing, and it's hard to say what came first, the chicken or the egg. Was I in poor spirits because I hadn't slept, or couldn't I sleep because I was in poor spirits? Either way, Shoestring was to blame. I looked at May resting so peacefully and thought how unfair it was. It was wrong of her to give away what didn't belong to her; more than wrong – it was criminal, and there she was sleeping like a baby whereas I, completely innocent, was wide awake and troubled.

I hopped to the mantelpiece to try and get some perspective on the matter but my thoughts kept going round in circles. Finally I could stand it no longer. I launched myself from my perch, swerved past the bedstead and headed out the open window. By then I'd changed my mind about warning Shoestring about that wretched card. I wanted my mirror back and that was all there was to it.

◇◇◇◇◇◇◇◇◇◇◇◇◇◇◇◇◇◇◇◇◇◇◇◇◇◇◇◇◇◇◇◇◇◇◇◇◇◇◇◇◇◇◇◇◇◇◇◇◇◇◇◇◇◇◇◇◇◇◇◇◇◇◇

FLYING WAS SOMETHING METROPOLIS DIDN'T do often. She'd flap around the Luck Palace if there wasn't a shoulder to ride on. She'd hop along the banister and sometimes slide down it if she needed to pay Mr Goldfiend a visit in the shop, and when she went out it was usually on May's shoulder. It wasn't that Metropolis disliked flying, it was just that she never had the need to do it. As she flew over the rooftops on the far side of Viva Street she realised she was out of practice.

Cadenza Towers was not far as the crow flies but it took Metropolis a long time to get there. The sun came up and the day was well underway by the time she arrived. She was out of breath and her wings ached.

When she landed on the wall Franko looked up, surprised. He was still cleaning up from the night before.

'Where's May?' he asked.

'Sleeping. I came by myself. Is Shoestring in?'

'Long gone,' Franko told her. 'They left at dawn. They'd be halfway to Riddley by now.'

'How far's that?'

'Too far for an old bird like you to fly.'

'I'm not old.' Metropolis put her beak in the air. She considered flapping down and taking a triangular-shaped piece out of his ear to teach him a lesson, but decided to save her energy.

'See you,' she squawked, trying to make her take-off look effortless.

I T WAS MADNESS TO ATTEMPT TO FLY SO FAR.
  At my age it was pure folly, especially when I'd hardly
slept. I'm a bird who likes her home comforts and there
I was, lost in the dark wood. Yes, lost! Night had fallen.
There was no sign of the troupe. It was too late to try and fly
home, even if I knew the way. May would be worried about
me. She would be frantic.

I hopped up into a tree and tried to settle myself. It was a long time since I'd been in a tree at night. In fact, I'd never been in one, not since I hatched. I sighed and tried not to think of the dangers, the creatures of the dark — cats and foxes and owls; when you're old and weak you can fall prey to myriad hazards.

I fluffed up my feathers to keep warm and I was drifting off to sleep when I heard a rush of wings. The wind from them lifted my crest. I opened one eye and saw a flash of white. I blinked and stared as a white bird landed in the tree behind me.

'Metropolis.' Its call was soft and whispery. The bird flew a short distance away then hovered as if it was waiting for me to follow. So I did. And that is something I regret to this day.

# CHAPTER SIX

# A WHITE BIRD

THE TROUPE MADE GOOD TIME ON THEIR first day's travel. They expected to stay at Riddley but as Grimwade's horse, Haul, showed no signs of tiring by the time they reached the town, they continued on until dusk. When they reached a clearing in the forest they stopped and set up their tents. There was a stream nearby and Lobe asked his daughters to get some water for Haul.

'Sylvie, come and help us,' Violet said, and the three girls headed off.

'Do you do everything together?' Sylvie asked.

'Everything.'

'Do you ever argue?'

'Never. We always agree, don't we, Daisy?'

'We do,' Daisy replied. 'We always see …'

'…eye to eye.' The twins faced each other. They linked little fingers and laughed.

'I wish I had a sister,' Sylvie said.

'We'll be your sisters!' the girls cried.

Sylvie couldn't believe her luck. She'd always wanted a sister and now she had two of them.

By the time the girls returned with the water, Grimwade had cooked one of his best dishes to celebrate their first night on the road.

'Tomorrow we'll get up early and begin practising,' said Shoestring. 'That's what we'll do every day.' Already he was loving his life on the road. He looked around at his friends and felt like the luckiest boy in the world.

After dinner everyone sat by the fire. Lovegrove finished stitching Sylvie's belt.

'Let's see how it fits.' She held it out and Sylvie stood up and lifted her arms.

'I had this belt when Lovegrove came,' she told the Dittos. 'I think my mother made it.'

'Where's your mother?' Daisy and Violet asked.

Sylvie didn't know. 'Maybe one day I'll find her,' she said. 'Lovegrove's my mother now.'

The belt fitted perfectly. There was even room to grow. Sylvie put it on over her pyjamas and when she took out her book and sat down between the twins, they squealed with delight when they saw the cover.

'That's our favourite story,' they cried. 'We know it off by heart.'

'I loved it when KidGlovz saved Shoestring's life.' Daisy flipped through the book looking for the page.

Shoe looked over her shoulder. 'Kid saved my life and I saved his. That's why we'll always be friends. We look younger there.'

'We *were* younger,' Kid said.

'So it's a true story then?' Lobe asked.

Kid nodded.

'My favourite bit is when you got back together with Lovegrove and Hugo.' Violet turned to the end of the book.

'That was my favourite bit!' Kid laughed.

She went to the start and recited the opening without looking.

*'There is a town in the mountains not far from here where people lock their pianos on the night of the full moon. It makes no difference – the keys move up and down and the air is filled with wild music.*

*'Someone once thought they saw a white bird flying between the trees,'* Daisy continued. *'But the truth of the matter is that it's not a bird that flies on the night of the full moon but a pair of white gloves—'*

'"I know this because they used to belong to me."' Kid finished the sentence.

'Do you ever miss those gloves, Kid?' Sylvie asked.

'Never,' Kid replied, stroking Hugo's shaggy ears. 'They brought me nothing but trouble. I've got a new life now.'

Lovegrove stood up. 'It's getting late,' she said. 'Sylvie, it's bedtime for you. Shoe will tuck you in.'

*What a perfect night,* Shoestring thought as he took Sylvie's hand. *Every night will be like this.*

THE INSIDE OF THE WAGON WAS COSY. The moon shone through the window and when Sylvie asked for the usual bedtime story, Shoe cupped his hands against the glass and made a shadow on the wall.

The shadow was good, he thought, not quite Hugo but certainly a dog. Sylvie clapped her hands and laughed. Both of them were so intent on the shadow they didn't notice Metropolis when she landed on the tailgate and poked her head under the canvas that covered the back of the wagon.

She looked at the shadow, then her beak dropped open: a second larger shadow appeared beside it. The shadow was also a dog but it was huge and fierce. Sylvie gasped and clutched Shoestring's arm.

'What's happening?' she cried.

THE LITTLE GIRL WAS TERRIFIED AND SO was I. Macaws are sensitive birds. Some may say they have a nervous disposition, and when a bird is tired and full of fright she can imagine all sorts of things. I closed my eyes and tried to still my beating heart but when I opened them again the shadow was still there. I'm not sure if it was a man or a goat.

'Who are you?' Shoestring cried. '*What* are you?'

'I'm just a shadow on the wall but I've come to offer you something truly marvellous.'

The girl let out a frightened cry and pointed to the window. 'Look, gloves!'

I turned my head. A pair of gloves was hovering at the glass.

'That's exactly what I'm offering,' the shadow said. 'A pair of gloves, gloves that will point the way for you, gloves that will find whatever you're looking for and bring you whatever you desire. All you have to do is try them on.'

'I don't want them,' Shoe gasped. 'Go away! You're scaring Sylvie!'

When Shoestring said that, the goat-man shadow came apart and the gloves flew off. Yes, flew — just like a bird! Sylvie burst into tears and Shoestring put his arm around her.

'It's all right,' he said. 'They're gone.'

I ducked my head back out from under the canvas and watched the gloves flap away, disappearing into the trees. The sight unnerved me and I was trembling so much my beak chattered. I hopped out of the way as Lovegrove and the others came running. They soon had Sylvie and Shoestring sitting by the fire bundled up in blankets. Shoestring was white as a ghost.

'What did the gloves look like?' Lovegrove asked.

'I don't know. I hardly saw them. I was looking at the shadow.'

'Were they like the gloves Kid used to wear?' the twins wanted to know.

'Bigger,' Shoestring whispered.

'Were they like the gloves in your dream?' Kid asked.

I could see he was worried; they all were.

Shoestring shrugged. I was about to stick my beak in and describe the gloves when little Sylvie beat me to it.

'They were large and white,' she said, drying her eyes. 'And they were stitched with shiny silver thread.'

As she spoke something rustled in the bushes behind me.

'*Metropolis.*' Again I heard that soft call. There was movement, a white blur, as the gloves flew off. Don't ask me why I followed. Something drew me after them.

The gloves didn't fly fast; I think they wanted me to keep up. They winged their way along a track between the trees and picked up speed when they reached open country. To my surprise I found that I could fly as fast as they could. Perhaps it was the night air or the full moon – I seemed to be gathering energy as I went along.

I watched them swoop down the chimney of a farmhouse.

Suddenly the air was full of crazy music. Some mad person was thumping at a piano. It was a terrible sound, the sort of music that could send you out of your tree. I flew down onto a windowsill and peered through the glass.

The gloves were playing, pounding out the notes, and the noise had woken the owners of the house. They stood bewildered in their nightwear, then stared in horror as the gloves made fists and crashed down onto the keyboard, splitting it in half. The gloves swept towards the window. They smashed the glass and flew off into the night with me trailing behind them. I wasn't trying to chase them; they seemed to have some sort of power that drew me in their wake.

There was a village not far from the house and when the gloves reached it they went from door to door, knocking. Dogs raised their hackles and howled, then yelped and ran for cover when the gloves threw stones at them. People stared from doorways wondering what was happening and when one woman ran outside to look, the gloves slapped her face.

'Metropolis,' they called, as they flew away over the rooftops.

I've seen some bad characters in my day, but those gloves were the worst. I followed them as the moon moved across the sky and I watched what they did in stunned silence. They left a trail of destruction. They broke weathervanes and turned signposts in the wrong direction. They frightened cattle and pinched sleeping children. They pulled out a crop of corn and applauded the act. They seemed bent on doing as much damage as they could before the night was out and I was dragged in their slipstream.

We reached the outskirts of a town and the gloves found a house where the second floor was lit with party lights. The people inside were singing 'Happy Birthday'. The window was open and the gloves flew straight in. Again I perched on the sill and watched the gloves at work. They moved like the hands of a waiter, picking up the birthday cake and whisking it away from under the people's noses before hurling it out the window.

The gloves flew on with me trailing after them. I had no idea where they were heading. At times I saw the lights of houses far below. Once I saw a river winding in the moonlight. It was just on dawn when a mountain loomed ahead. The top was lost in cloud. The gloves climbed steeply, and when they flew over the summit I looked down and realised that I'd seen this place before. Immediately I let out a squawk and stopped flying.

'No, not here!'

The moment I cried out the gloves turned on me.

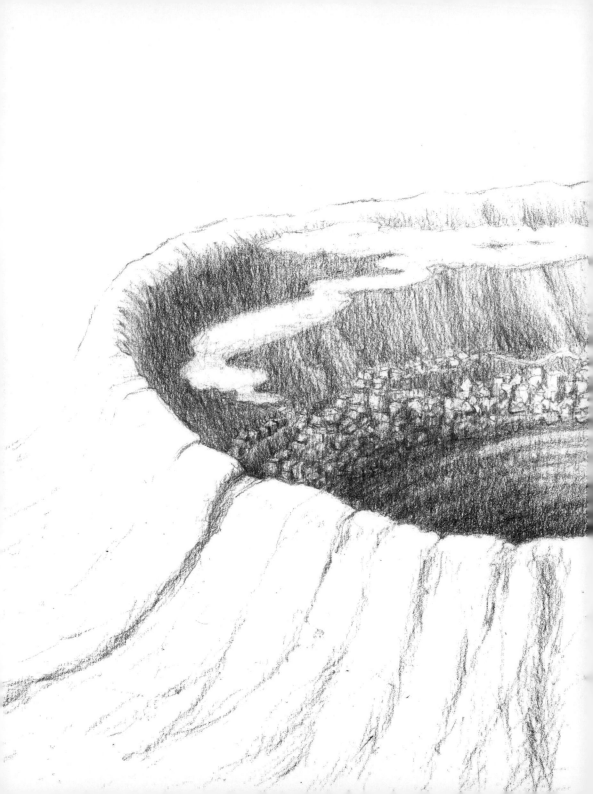

# PART TWO

# CHAPTER SEVEN

# LOST

SOMETIMES IF I'M OUT OF SORTS I TELL myself a story, a true story about a Fabulous Macaw who comes from a place called the Archipelago in a country of lush jungle swathed in mist. Her name is Metropolis. She has had three owners and lived three lives. Her first owner lived in a hut on the riverbank and was so clever he could see in the dark and move without making a sound. He possessed nothing except his wits, which were exceptionally sharp, and a pack of cards with pictures on them.

One night he drew out a card that showed a bird with glossy wings rising over a pile of gold. He slipped it back into the pack and walked deep into the forest, moving from tree to tree until he found one that felt right. He looked up into the canopy, then began climbing. When he reached the nest, all hell broke loose. A whole flock of macaws rose screeching and flapping. The man snatched an egg and was down from the tree and padding along the forest floor before the birds knew what had happened. He paused some distance away and listened until the flock settled and the only sound was a soft rustling noise like May makes when she's going through her wardrobe. Then he continued home, carrying the egg that was me with the greatest care.

When I hatched, my first owner crowed with such pride you'd have thought he laid the egg himself. He proceeded to teach me all he knew, card by card. I repeated everything he said until I knew the cards by heart. Then, when I was little more than a chick, he told me it was time to earn my keep.

He took me to a nearby town and we sat down in the marketplace. I perched on his shoulder as he shuffled his cards. He called me the Oracle Bird and before long a crowd had gathered. I soon understood what I had to do. I was clever, even then. When a person picked a card, it was my job to enlighten them as to its meaning. The person would then hand some gold to my owner. He was very pleased with me and I was glad to make him happy – after all, he was my mother, my father and my whole world; I followed him everywhere and I thought we would always be together.

One day my owner met a woman in the marketplace who came from a far country. She was wearing diamond earrings and a monocle with a gold rim. Two thickset men in dark glasses accompanied her. They stood on either side with their arms folded.

'Hear the Oracle Bird read the Cards of Life!' my master cried.

The woman shook her head. She said she already knew her future so there was no need for me to read the cards, but she watched me perform from the edge of the crowd. After some time she stepped forward. She handed my master more gold than I had ever seen and then, with one smooth movement, she scooped up the cards, and me with them. The cards went into her pocket and she tucked me under her arm. My master didn't protest and as she walked away I realised what had happened: I had been sold!

That woman, my second owner, is someone I'd prefer to forget. When I'm telling myself the story of my life I always pass quickly on to my third owner, May, Queen of Hearts. May is the finest person in this world. She rescued me from a fate worse than death and I love her dearly, even if we do have our differences.

<><><><><><><><><><><><><><><><><><><><><><><><><><><><><><><><><><><><><>

'SHE MUST BE HERE SOMEWHERE.'

May looked behind the curtains in the gaming room for the third time.

'Did you say something to offend her?' Ruby asked, as she lifted the piano lid and peered inside.

'I'm always offending her. She's so touchy. Now, where haven't we looked?'

They had searched the entire Luck Palace – the kitchen, the smoking room, the gaming room, the back room, the card parlour, the shop, all the bedrooms, the bathrooms and the workshop out the back where Mr Goldfiend and his apprentices made alterations to the jewellery and other goods that ended up in his hands.

'Have you checked your wardrobe?' Ruby asked.

'Of course.'

The wardrobe was the first place May had looked. It was one of Metropolis's favourite hiding spots; whenever she was upset she would conceal herself in its recesses, roosting among May's dresses, fans and feather boas.

'She's not there. She's not anywhere.' May flopped down on a couch. 'I'm going to give that bird a piece of my mind when she shows up!'

'You don't think she's gone out?' Ruby ventured.

'Out? Out where?'

May knew Metropolis better than anyone. They had been together since she was a girl and in all that time the macaw had rarely gone out on her own.

'Where's Lobe?' she asked. 'I'll ask him to listen for her.'

May was sure that Lobe would find Metropolis immediately. He'd pick up the sound of her breathing or the rustling of a wing feather.

'He hasn't been around today.' Ruby sat down next to May. 'Maybe she's been stolen.'

'Who would steal Metropolis?' May knew Ruby was a worrier. She'd always been that way.

'Metropolis might have been kidnapped,' the waitress said. 'A woman in your position has enemies.'

It was true. May had many devoted friends but she also had a few enemies, people who had gambled the shirts off their backs and blamed her for the loss.

'If Metropolis has been kidnapped I'll get a ransom note.' She looked up at the chandelier and sighed. It was morning and the sun shone through a crack in the curtains, making the crystal sparkle and send bright reflections across the wall. She thought of the mirror. 'I know what's happened,' she said. 'I bet she's gone to get her mirror back.'

I WOKE UP IN A CAGE COVERED WITH A THICK black cloth. There was a mirror dangling in front of me. It was nothing like my own. It was cracked and so covered in dust that I could barely see my outline. I was about to brush it clean to see what state I was in when someone spoke.

'Have you filled her water bowl?'

My heart thumped wildly. How long since I'd heard that voice? It must be forty years!

'Of course, Madam,' came a whispery reply.

A hand slipped under the cloth. It was old and bony but I knew by the rings on the fingers who it belonged to. It was Mistress Adamantine, also known as Marm. Her fingernails were long and shiny and they glittered in the darkness.

IT'S MARM!

She opened the door and when she clasped my legs and pulled me upside down from the cage I shrieked in terror and let out a string of curses that doesn't bear repeating.

'What a foul mouth you have, Metropolis. Curse all you like. It will do you no good.'

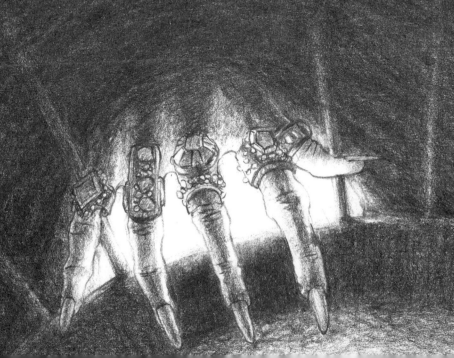

I flapped in panic until my wings were pinned. When I looked up I saw the gloves, one on each side of me, holding me tight. Above them was Marm's jewelled hand and beyond that, her ghastly face peering down at me. I dropped my head and stared at the floor. The tiles were covered in dry leaves.

'Silence is golden,' she said. 'Let's make it permanent. Take her voice!'

'Yes, Madam. Where shall I put it?'

'In the strong room.'

The gloves released my wings. Before I had time to flap they were around my throat, squeezing hard.

I must have fainted. When I came to my senses I was back in the cage. One of my feathers had fallen out and lay on the floor. My throat felt terrible. I could still feel the fingers of the gloves closing around it.

Marm's hand poked through the door. She scattered a few sunflower seeds then picked up the feather. I tried to squawk but I couldn't make a sound.

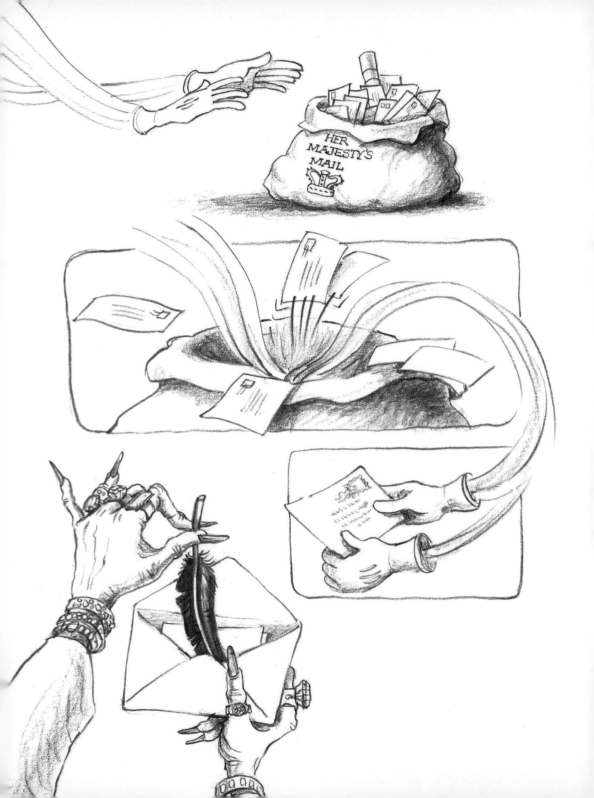

A WEEK WENT BY AT THE LUCK PALACE and there was no sign of Metropolis. May was annoyed.

It was difficult running the place without her. May had nobody to help in the gaming room, nobody with whom to discuss the evening's clientele and, worst of all, she had to count the night's takings herself, a job Metropolis usually did because of the macaw's facility with numbers.

Each day May was up until ten doing the books, when she should have been in bed by dawn.

'Talk about inconsiderate,' she said one morning as she closed the ledger and handed it to Mr Goldfiend. 'Metropolis has left me in the lurch.'

Just then Ruby came in with a letter.

Dear May,

Sorry for leaving without giving notice. The girls wanted to be in Shoestring's troupe, so what could I do? I hope you can find someone else for the door.

Regards
Lobe Ditto

A small black feather fell out of the envelope and May bit her lip. It really was too much, she thought. Metropolis hadn't even asked Lobe to send her regards. She'd just slipped in a bit of down, a breast feather to let May know where she was.

Ruby held it up. 'Metropolis? she asked.

'Who else? She's with the troupe. I suppose she wants to be a star like Shoestring.'

May studied the postmark on the envelope then immediately put pen to paper, addressing the letter to Ace, King of the Cards, c/o The Troupe of Marvels, via Riddley.

# The Tour

GRIMWADE SAT AT THE DOOR OF THE TENT selling tickets. 'We'll have to get more printed,' he said to Ace. 'At this rate we'll run out in a week.'

'Standing room only,' he yelled, as the crowds poured in.

Out the back, KidGlovz was tying a ringmaster's hat on Hugo. The dog didn't seem to mind. He wagged his tail and looked to Lovegrove, waiting to go on.

Shoestring was halfway down a ladder that led to a platform high above the ring. He jumped into the safety net then bounced out of it and landed on the ground. Then he slipped outside.

The Dittos were standing by the back wall of the tent and Lobe was adjusting their outfits.

'How do we look, Shoe?' they asked.

'Lovely,' he replied. 'Are you all set?'

Lobe lifted the tent flap and they peered in, watching the audience arrive.

'See that man in the checked jacket?' Lobe whispered.

The twins nodded.

'His stomach is rumbling like an avalanche. You can bet he's wishing he ate dinner before he came. Got that?'

'Yes, Dad,' they said.

'…and that lady sitting in the front row with the blue handbag… I heard her arguing with her husband as she left home. She said some terrible things and she'll be worrying about it.'

Violet was momentarily distracted as Lovegrove stepped into the ring and welcomed the audience. It didn't matter. Only one of them needed to hear what Lobe was saying.

*The Dittos are a good act to start the show,* Shoestring thought as he stood by the tent flap watching the crowd.

'Ladies and gentlemen, it is my pleasure to introduce you to an evening of wonders and delights!' Lovegrove announced. Hugo barked loudly and everyone cheered. 'An evening of music, magic and imagination. Tonight you will see feats of skill and daring. You will witness acts that can hardly be believed…'

'… and those two boys at the back – the ones whispering to each other…' Lobe continued. Violet gave him her attention.

'What are they saying, Dad?' she asked.

'They're talking about a girl called Eleanor Bright.'

'Our first act features two talented young ladies.' Lovegrove addressed the audience. 'Daisy and Violet. What a combination, ladies and gentlemen – they sing, they dance, they hear each other's thoughts. Put your hands together for the amazing Ditto Twins!'

Lobe stepped back. 'Good luck, girls. You're on!'

The twins did a medley, singing and dancing and moving smoothly from one song to the next, accompanied by KidGlovz on accordion. One moment they were tap dancing and the next they did balletic pirouettes. When their final song ended in the splits, the girls arched backwards and put their heads on their heels. They were strong and supple and they bent themselves into impossible shapes that made the audience gasp with delight.

The twins came out of their grasshopper pose and took a bow. Violet put a blindfold on her sister and spun her around so she was facing the back wall of the tent. Then she wandered into the audience and, with a sweet smile, borrowed a gentleman's watch.

'What have I got, Daisy?' she asked, holding it up. She closed her eyes and sent the thought to her sister. *It's a watch, Daisy. I think it's gold and it's five minutes late.*

Daisy put her hand on her head as if what she was about to do required great concentration.

'I see something round…' she began. 'Something small and round. I believe it's a watch. A gold watch. It appears to be a little slow. Five minutes, I think.'

The audience applauded. Violet returned the watch and plucked a rose from the man's buttonhole.

'I see a flower,' Daisy said. 'A pink flower. It could be a rose.'

'Not only do they read each other's thoughts, ladies and gentlemen,' Lovegrove said, 'they can read yours as well.'

Daisy took off her blindfold. She scanned the audience until her gaze rested on a man in a checked jacket. 'You sir, in the third row from the front…' She closed her eyes and frowned. 'You wish you had eaten…'

'…before you came out tonight,' Violet finished the sentence.

'It's true!' the man said, surprised.

'And those boys up the back.' Daisy pointed towards the entrance. 'Their heads are full of…'

'…a girl called…Eleanor Bright,' Violet declared.

The boys looked shocked and the crowd laughed.

'And, to the lady with the blue handbag.' Violet nodded to a woman in the front row. 'Don't worry about the fight you had with your husband before you left home, Madam. He's forgiven you.'

'That's extraordinary!' the woman cried.

SHOESTRING JOINED IN THE APPLAUSE WHEN the girls took their final bow. Ace was on next, dazzling the audience with his card tricks. Then came Grimwade with his drum solo and some heartfelt songs from his home, a village on the shores of Lake Ostinato. He sang with such feeling that several people reached for their handkerchiefs.

Sylvie followed Grimwade with a virtuoso violin solo. Then Grimwade played a drum roll and a hush fell over the audience.

*This is the best bit*, Shoestring thought as he climbed the ladder.

'And now, ladies and gentlemen, the act you have all been waiting for...' Lovegrove declared. 'Shoestring – The Boy Who Walks on Air!'

Shoestring loved hearing the sudden intake of breath as he stepped onto the rope. He loved it when he looked down and saw all the upturned faces. They made him think of coins, hundreds of coins scattered at his feet, more coins than he had ever taken when he was a pickpocket. And he wasn't stealing now, he was earning his keep. He loved the applause too, the rush and roar of it; if the rope hadn't been there he felt the applause could almost have held him up. Then, after the performance, everyone wanted to talk to him, to shake his hand and touch him to make sure he was real.

That night was no exception. People crowded around him after the show.

'You're brilliant,' they cried. 'You really are a marvel!'

'Where are you heading next?' somebody asked.

Shoestring smiled and shrugged. The troupe had been on the road for a month. They went wherever the breeze took them. If the road they were on forked, they flipped a coin to decide whether they would go left or right and when they reached a crossroads they threw two coins, one for north or south, then one for east or west. They followed rivers, back roads and byways, weaving their way across the country, and they were welcomed wherever they went.

Shoe loved the travelling life. Apart from that worrying incident on the first night, he felt the trip was charmed. He forgot about the gloves and the shadow he'd seen on the wall. His future was ahead of him and every time he performed he felt himself improving.

That evening he went to bed happy as always and the next morning he grew even happier, because a postman arrived with an envelope addressed to The Boy Who Walks on Air. Shoe couldn't read. He'd never learned how. He handed the envelope to Sylvie and she read the card inside. KidGlovz looked over her shoulder.

'The Festival of Marvels – and we're the Troupe of Marvels,' Sylvie said. 'What do you make of that?'

'It's meant to be!' Shoe declared.

To

MASTER SHOESTRING

You are invited to compete in the prestigious

◊ JUBILEE FESTIVAL OF MARVELS ◊

IN THE

Death-defying Fame and Fortune Award

FOR THE

WORLD'S LEADING HIGH WIRE ARTIST

1-4 APRIL

TOP PRIZES · HUGE AUDIENCES

Sylvie turned the invitation over and found a map on the back. The festival was on the other side of the country. 'Lovegrove, look at this.'

'The chance of a lifetime!' Lovegrove said, and they all agreed.

'He'll compete with the best in the world.' Ace looked proud.

Shoe wished he could write. He felt like telling May immediately. She'd be thrilled for him. She'd put the invitation on her mantelpiece.

He studied the picture. 'Death-defying – that's me!' He could see himself dancing on air, performing above the multitudes. He'd walk higher and further than anyone had ever done before. 'I'll win the award. I know I will. There's nothing surer. I've got to start practising.'

'You're already practising,' Kid said. 'We all practise every morning.'

'I mean really practising.'

A few days later Shoe found the perfect opportunity. They stopped at a campsite near a large town. It was a grassy spot on the edge of a gorge.

'Excellent,' said Shoestring, as he looked over the drop. He waited until Lovegrove and the others went off to put up posters, then strung up his rope.

D ON'T ASK ME HOW LONG I SPENT IN THAT cage. Weeks? Months? I couldn't tell you. I didn't know my nights from my days or my east from my west. I was stranded in time and I fell into a dark place from which I never expected to return. There was no sound except for Marm's echoing footsteps and occasionally a soft brushing noise as if someone was rubbing their hands together. My water bowl was filled, and now and then I was fed, and as I languished in the cage the past I thought I'd left behind came rushing back to meet me.

I'd met Marm before, you see. She was my second owner. She'd bought me in the marketplace and as we travelled to the distant country she had come from, I resolved never to speak again. Words were my undoing. They were my gift, my skill, my display, but look where they had brought me. If I had been an ordinary macaw uttering no more than the occasional raucous cry, that woman would never have noticed me. The fact that I was dumped in a gilded cage in the entrance hall of her grand mansion and told to report on the servants who, poor wretches, were no more than slaves, only strengthened my resolve.

When Marm realised I wouldn't speak she thought she had somehow been tricked. She peered through the bars of my cage brandishing a black feather duster.

'You wretched bird,' she hissed. 'I should wring your neck. I should have you plucked. I should roast you for dinner.'

I squawked in fright.

'At least you're not useless,' she said. 'If you see anyone stealing, you're to raise the alarm. If you don't do your job, you'll end up like this.'

She hit the cage with the duster and for a moment all I could see was a cloud of feathers that had come from some poor dead bird, possibly a macaw like myself. Then she swept up the spiral staircase to her tower, leaving me alone in the entrance hall.

I sat hunched in my little prison. The Cards of Life were

scattered at the bottom of my cage like so much litter. I didn't have the heart to read them – I knew my future was hopeless.

Now I was back in exactly the same situation: the same cage, same house, and same mistress.

I tried to force my head through the bars but as you may know the *Macoa macaurus fabulosa* has an exceptionally large brain and a skull commodious enough to house it, so my attempt came to nothing. I did get my beak through, though, and I had a peck at the lock. It was the same lock that had secured me all those years ago, the only change being that it was now rusty and likely to be stiff. I tried to spit on it, hoping my saliva would seep inside and grease the internal mechanism, but my throat was dry. Next I tried to bite through the bars but they were made of iron and even a beak as powerful as mine had little effect. Was it any wonder I fell into a despond?

With nothing else to occupy my mind I found myself dwelling on the past. I remembered the maids. They were barely fed, and if they so much as looked at one of Marm's priceless diamonds they would be locked in the strongroom or sent down her mine. Marm's guards ate three meals a day. She allowed them food because they had to be strong to bully the rest of the staff. It was easy to see the pecking order: Marm was on top, her son was next – after them came the guards, and the maids were at the bottom of the heap.

*Don't think about it, Metropolis,* I told myself.

I rocked on my perch and tried to come back to the present.

I pictured my life at the Luck Palace but it seemed very far away, and when I found myself reciting the names of precious stones I knew it was the first sign of madness.

Moonstone, serpentine, amethyst, emerald... Back then I knew them all. I could tell the difference between tanzanite, turquoise and sapphire, between bloodstone, red topaz, ruby and the most precious stone of all, the fire diamond, which Marm called the Eye of the Dragon. This stone was kept in her tower. Sometimes a stray breeze would carry her voice down the stairs and I would hear her muttering endearments to that diamond. 'My darling one, my dazzlement, light of my life...'

'Metropolis, wake up!' I said to myself.

Footsteps were coming towards me, Marm's heeled boots on the tiled floor of the entrance hall. Light fell on the bottom of my cage as she lifted a corner of the cloth.

I heard her laugh, a thin wheezing sound. 'Not long now,' she muttered.

# CHAPTER NINE

# THE GLOVES

'NO, SHOE. YOU CAN'T WALK ACROSS THERE. The gap's too wide for the net.' Lovegrove stood looking over the gorge. Shoestring had fixed his rope to a tree on the far side.

'I don't care about the safety net,' he said. 'It's more exciting without it.'

'What if you fall?'

'I won't. I'm sure of it.'

THAT NIGHT BY THE CAMPFIRE, SHOESTRING was in high spirits. It was a beautiful evening. Grimwade was singing as he washed the dishes, accompanied by Kid's accordion. Ace and Lobe were playing cards and the girls had their noses in the book. Lovegrove was giving Hugo a brush and each time Grimwade finished a song the dog raised his head and barked for more, making everyone laugh.

'What a life,' Shoe said. 'Tonight was fantastic. The show just gets better and better.' He stood up and smiled at the moon. 'I'm off to bed.'

Shoestring crawled into the tent and lay down on top of the blankets in his white suit. There was room to stretch out as Kid was still outside with the others.

*It was a victory, performing without the net*, he thought. *It was exhilarating.* He closed his eyes and remembered how it felt. 'Thrilling,' he whispered to himself.

'I'll show you thrilling!'

'Kid?' Shoestring sat up with a start. The voice didn't sound like it belonged to KidGlovz, but someone was outside the tent. He looked about. Moonlight shone through the canvas and suddenly he saw a hand with two fingers raised in a V-for-victory sign. Then a second hand joined the first and there was the shape of a man's head, the same shadow Shoestring had seen on the first night of their tour.

'I'll show you thrilling,' the shadow repeated.

'What?' Shoestring stared.

'Try on the gloves and you'll know what it is to be truly thrilled.'

'What do you mean?'

The shadow came apart and the gloves disappeared. A moment later they were inside the tent.

They were empty gloves. Shoestring could see there was nothing inside them, yet they seemed full of themselves. Both hands hovered before him, palm up with the fingers spread. Then they flipped over so the openings gaped in his direction, as if daring him to try them on.

For a second Shoe remembered that dream he'd had the night before he left Cadenza and his heart began to race. He took a deep breath. *I'm not scared*, he told himself. *Not after tonight, not after walking across a sheer drop*. He thought of the crowds and felt their adulation. He heard the roar of approval.

My hands are tingling...

'It can't hurt to try them on,' he said.

It was a strange feeling. Shoestring could hear Kid playing accordion. He could hear Grimwade singing and the others laughing and talking, but the sounds seemed far away. He flexed his fingers. The gloves were tight but not too tight. He felt the power in them. It was running up his arms. He crawled out of the tent and, putting his hands in his pockets, walked from the campsite.

'Hey, Shoe. Where are you going?' Kid called out, still playing.

'Just for a walk.'

He hurried down the road that led to the town and when he saw the lights of the first house, he began running. It wasn't late; people were still about. He saw a group sitting at a table outside a restaurant.

'It's the boy from the show,' a man called out. 'Bravo, lad! Your act was spectacular. Will you join us?'

Shoestring thanked the man, but declined. He felt he had something important to do but he wasn't sure what it was. He continued on his way and when he reached a shop window he paused at his reflection in the glass. He looked good in his white suit, and the gloves completed his outfit. He wished May could see him and thought how far he'd come since he was a thief and common pickpocket.

'Look at me now – The Boy Who Walks on Air!'

A smartly dressed man passed by. Shoestring noticed the fellow had a wallet poking from his back pocket and, before he knew what was happening, the wallet was in his hand. He hadn't meant to steal it – in fact, he hadn't even noticed himself doing it. *I should give it back*, he thought, and with that, the gloves tightened on his hands. 'Ouch!'

The man was halfway down the street by the time Shoestring caught up with him. 'You dropped your wallet.'

'Thank you. What an honest boy.'

Honest? Shoestring had never been called honest before. The man continued walking and Shoe was distracted by the smell of roasting nuts wafting from a street stall ahead.

He could see bags of hot nuts sitting on a table. A woman was cooking them over some coals. She turned her back for a moment and before he knew it the gloves slipped from his hands. They moved like lightning, grabbing a bag and tossing it in his direction. He caught it and hurried around a corner.

'I didn't steal them,' he said as he put one in his mouth. A second later the gloves were back. It was confusing, but the nuts were delicious. He felt like laughing with surprise. Shoe had almost finished the bag when two people walked past, a man and his son. They looked wealthy. The boy wore a fine scarf and a tailored coat and Shoestring couldn't help noticing his impressive head of hair.

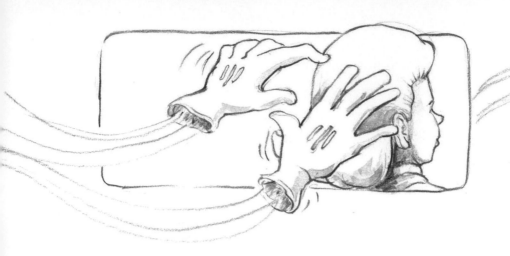

The gloves moved too fast to see and in a moment the boy was bald as an old man. His face crumpled and he began to cry like a much younger child.

Shoestring stood in shock. Then he ran his fingers through his own hair. It felt thick and long, nothing like his usual haircut. The father's mouth dropped open for a moment before his bewilderment turned to anger.

'I don't know what confounded nonsense you're up to, young man, but you're not getting away with it!'

*What* am *I up to?* Shoestring asked himself. He checked his reflection in his mirror and he had to admit the new hair suited him.

'This is absurd,' the boy's father yelled. 'It's an abomination. You scoundrel. You thief!'

He grabbed Shoestring by the collar and began hauling him along the street. 'You can explain your unnatural act to the local constabulary.'

'The police?' Shoe's heart began to thump inside his chest. What could he say to defend himself? That the gloves did it? He looked at the man and wished he could speak like him, using big important words and saying them with such authority. The moment he had that thought the gloves shot through the air.

'Are you accusing me of confiscating your son's head of hair? I have never in all my life met with such a ludicrous suggestion.' The words rolled off Shoe's tongue as if he owned them. 'Unhand me. Have you taken leave of your senses?'

The man held Shoestring in one hand and his throat with the other. He opened and closed his mouth but nothing came out. By the time he reached the police station his face was red and a purple vein pulsed in his forehead.

'He stole my hair. I swear it!' The boy pointed at Shoe and his father nodded emphatically. His lips were clamped together now and he held Shoe tight.

The policeman shook his head and took a form from the drawer of his desk.

'Name?' he asked.

'Shoestring.'

The policeman looked up. 'Not Shoestring – The Boy Who Walks on Air?'

Shoestring nodded. 'Yes, that's me.'

The policeman touched his eyebrow with the top of his pen and smiled.

'I heard the show was spectacular. Are you performing tomorrow night?'

'Same time, same place.' Shoestring's fingers whipped two tickets from his top pocket and held them out. He stared at them for a second, wondering how they got there, then offered them to the policeman. 'Please accept these free tickets.'

The policeman turned to the boy's father.

'Let him go,' he ordered. 'What's this nonsense about?

The man looked as if he might burst, but said nothing. Shoestring, however, was not lost for words.

'An unfortunate misunderstanding, Constable. Nothing more.'

He tried not to show his surprise at the ease with which he spoke. The man gaped, his eyes bulging, and his son clung to him and sobbed. Shoe felt a twinge of guilt.

*It doesn't matter*, he told himself. *Better than going to jail.*

His heart was beating fast as he left the police station. Shoestring had a great fear of the police and rarely saw them at close quarters. He thought how brave he'd been, chatting away like that. How clever he was to offer the man the tickets. The gloves had done it, of course. The gloves had allowed him to steal and get off scot-free. It was astonishing!

He walked quickly up the street. The night was chilly and when he passed a shop with a display of scarves in the window, one caught his eye. It was deep blue with a pattern of silver stars and it was made of the finest wool. There was a flurry of white and in an instant the scarf was around his neck. The gloves moved so quickly he didn't see them leave his hands.

*These gloves are thrilling*, he thought. *The shadow was right.*

He headed home, hoping Kid was still awake.

# CHAPTER TEN

# A Promise

ALL WAS QUIET AT THE CAMPSITE WHEN Shoestring returned. Lobe was in his hammock strung between the trees and Ace was snoring in his swag beneath the wagon. The fire was out except for a few coals that glowed in the dark.

Shoestring took off the gloves and put them in his pocket as he crept past the fireplace. He slunk into the tent and found KidGlovz waiting up for him.

'Where have you been, Shoe? What's happened to your hair?' Kid noticed the scarf. 'And where did you get that?' he asked.

Shoestring put his finger to his lips.

'Kid, something amazing happened,' he whispered. 'Come outside. I don't want to wake the others.'

He led Kid away from the camp and they sat on the edge of the gorge with their legs dangling over the side. Shoe took out a crumpled paper bag and offered Kid a nut.

'I didn't steal these,' he said. 'I just wanted them and in

an instant they were in my hands. It was the same with this.'
He ran his fingers through his new, long hair, then grabbed
a handful and tugged as if he thought it might come off. It
didn't.

Kid looked at him in bewilderment.

'It's hard to explain. I just had to want it and it was mine,'
Shoe said. 'I thought I was gone when the boy's father hauled
me to the police station. That fellow was full of himself. He
talked like a judge and I knew whatever I said the policeman
wouldn't believe me. I wished I could speak like him and then
it happened! The words just came out of my mouth. I didn't
know what I was going to say next but it all sounded perfect.'

Shoe knew he was babbling but he wanted Kid to
understand. 'It was the gloves,' he said, and taking them from
his pocket, he looked at them in admiration. The moon was
sinking behind the trees but the gloves shone brightly. They
seemed to have their own light.

KidGlovz's heart missed a beat. He remembered wearing
those gloves. He'd watched his fingers run up and down the
keyboard, amazed at the music.

'Throw them away, Shoe. No good will come of them.'

'Why? They're precious. They're magic. They can get me
whatever I want.' Shoestring held the gloves out in front of
him. 'You had them. You should know—'

Kid feared for his friend. 'Drop them, Shoe. Drop them
into the gorge and let that be the end of it.'

'I can't.'

'Please, Shoe.' Kid was begging.

Shoestring put the gloves on his lap. He stroked the back of one of them.

'It's as if they're alive,' he whispered. 'You wouldn't throw a living thing into the gorge. It'd be cruel. And such a terrible waste.' He placed one of the gloves on Kid's knee. 'A despicable, wanton and profligate waste!' he declared.

Kid couldn't help giggling. 'Is that how you talked?'

Shoe nodded. His shoulders were shaking as he tried to hold in his laughter.

'I *will* get rid of them, Kid,' he said. 'Just not tonight. I'll keep them for a day or so. You had them for years. It's only fair.'

Kid was doubtful. 'Do you promise?' he asked.

'If you swear not to tell the others. Let's keep it a secret just between you and me.'

The two boys shook hands and when Shoestring put the gloves back in his pocket, Kid wondered why he had agreed. He stood up and walked to the wagon, returning with a lamp and a pair of scissors. 'I'm going to cut your hair,' he said. 'If the others see you looking like that they'll want to know what happened.'

Shoestring took out the mirror that hung around his neck and watched as Kid snipped off the long, flowing locks. *A pity,* he thought. *I liked that hair.*

'BREAKFAST. ROLL UP. ROLL UP!'

Grimwade flipped the last pancake and Shoestring was holding out his plate when Lobe came up to him.

'A word in your ear, boy,' he said quietly. 'You wouldn't hide anything from the troupe, would you?'

'No. Why?' Shoestring looked Lobe straight in the eye. He liked Lobe. He'd known him all his life but he didn't feel like speaking with him right now.

*That's the trouble with living closely like this*, he thought. *People can't mind their own business.*

Grimwade slipped the pancake onto Shoe's plate and the boy bolted it down.

'Got to go, Lobe,' he said. 'It's time for practice.'

By the time Shoestring had checked his rope everyone was hard at work. Cards flew from Ace's hands. The Dittos had limbered up and were upside down, trying a quickstep on the seat of the wagon with their tap shoes on their hands while Kid played double time. Sylvie had her violin tucked under her chin. She was listening to Lovegrove's instructions. 'A little more accent on the entry to the third movement, Sylvie. And keep the vibrato low.'

Shoestring was about to step onto his rope when a postman arrived. May's letter had been readdressed so many times there was no more room on the envelope.

Dear Ace,

I hope the troupe is doing well and Shoestring is staying out of trouble. Please thank Lobe for his considerate letter. Tell him not to worry about the job. It will be here waiting for him when he gets back.

It's a pity Metropolis couldn't find it within herself to say hello — after all, we've been together for nearly forty years. What sort of act is she doing? I suppose she's reading the cards.

She's probably trying to upstage Shoestring. I'm disappointed in her, Ace. She left without a word and it's difficult running the Palace without her. I suppose she needed to spread her wings but I can't for the life of me think why she would go on tour. She hates camping. It reminds her of the long years she and I spent on the road. Anyway, look after her and give my love to Shoestring, the twins and your good self. I hope the crowds are loving your card tricks.

Your May, Queen of Hearts xxx

Ace read the letter twice, once to himself and once aloud. It worried him.

'May loves that bird,' he said. 'I hope nothing's happened to her. I think we'd better go home.'

'Home? But we're on tour. We're heading for the festival!'

Shoestring felt a bit mean saying that. He knew how upset May would be if she lost Metropolis. He didn't care about the macaw – as far as he was concerned she was a bad-tempered creature who tried to rule the roost – but he felt for May.

'She'll turn up,' he said. 'She's probably sulking somewhere.'

'Do you want to go back, Ace?' Lovegrove asked, concerned.

'I'll think on it, Lovegrove.'

'While you're deciding, perhaps we should move on to the next town,' she suggested.

'But people are dying to see me walk over the gorge again,' Shoestring cried.

'That's what I'm worried about. I've told you before that I don't want you performing without a net.'

'I'll second that,' Ace said. 'Let's move on to a safer spot.'

Shoestring was about to protest when Lovegrove raised her hand.

'No arguments,' she said. 'If anything happened to you May would never forgive me.'

'Or me,' said Ace.

Shoe thought of the policeman who was expecting to see the show that night.

'But I've already sold tickets,' he said.

'Too bad,' Ace told him. 'Everyone start packing. We'll hit the road as soon as we can.'

The troupe packed up and continued on their way. By the time they arrived in the next place and set up camp next to a river, Ace had made up his mind.

'This will be our last show,' he said. 'Tomorrow we'll head home.'

Shoe bit his lip. He felt torn in two directions. He was sorry for May but he wanted to go to the festival. He wanted it badly. He put everything out of his mind and concentrated on his performance.

That night he was spectacular. He asked Sylvie to play triple-time; he did three double backflips instead of two and ended his act with a daring run of somersaults. He worked so hard on the rope he wore himself out, and after the show he went straight to bed.

He hardly slept. He dreamed the troupe was heading back to Cadenza and his heart was so heavy that Haul could barely drag the wagon. He'd miss the Festival of Marvels and he wouldn't win the Death-Defying Fame and Fortune Award. And all because of Metropolis. He'd never liked that bird.

In his dream he sat hunched on the back of the wagon with his head in his hands. They were still far from Cadenza but he could hear May crying as if he was in the Luck Palace. Ruby was trying to comfort her.

'I'm sure she'll come back, May. Please don't cry.'

'Something terrible has happened to her. I know it.' May's voice was broken and she gave a heaving sob. The sound made Shoestring's chest hurt. He wanted to hug her and tell her that everything would be all right.

The sound of the crying faded and all Shoestring could hear in his dream was the clip-clop of Haul's hoofs on the road. He was trying to think what to do when a voice drifted through his mind – *That's exactly what I'm offering…A pair of gloves that will point the way for you, gloves that will find whatever you're looking for and bring you whatever you desire…*

*Snap!* Someone clicked their fingers next to his ear and he woke with a start. He sat up and opened his eyes.

'Kid?' he asked. His friend was asleep beside him.

Shoe saw something white flash past; then, seconds later, a shadow appeared on the tent wall.

'You again!'

'My dear friend, your sleep is troubled. How can I be of assistance?' The shadow's voice was softer than he remembered. It took on the tone of an obsequious servant. 'Your wish is my command.'

'Did you say the gloves could find whatever I'm looking for?' Shoestring whispered.

'Most certainly,' the shadow replied.

'Could they find a lost bird?'

'With no problem at all. Just hold out your hands.'

Shoestring hesitated. He had promised Kid he'd throw the gloves away, but there was May to think of. In his mind he saw her with red-rimmed eyes, and a face puffy from crying. He took a deep breath then poked his hands through the tent flap. The gloves slipped onto them.

THE NEXT MORNING SHOESTRING WAS nowhere to be found. It looked as though he'd left in a hurry. His blankets were strewn along the ground and his rope was still in his tent.

# CHAPTER ELEVEN

#  Marm

'**M**Y PRECIOUS ONE, MY SWEET AND shining star...'

I cringed at the sound of Marm's voice.

It drifted down from the top of the stairs the same as it had so many years before.

I sensed the place had changed since then. There was no sound of the maids and no sound of anyone coming and going. In the old days diamond traders would come to do business and the managers from Marm's mine would be at the gate every morning to receive the orders she'd shout from the tower. Now there was just the sound of the wind outside and occasionally the noise of dry leaves blowing across the floor. Once or twice I heard her speaking to her guards, but mostly there was silence.

'My dearest, my dazzlement, my darling brightness...'

Marm still loved the fire diamond. She always had. The only thing she loved more than that red stone was her son, Jack Diamond. The thought of him made me shudder. He was a bad egg if ever there was one.

Back then Jack was set to inherit the House of Diamonds. He already had his own private collection and I suspected he was feathering his nest by helping himself to his mother's stones when she went away on her trading trips. If the mistress noticed that a diamond had gone missing, a servant was blamed. Jack smiled whenever this happened, revealing the glittering zircon with which he had replaced his right eye tooth.

My days at the House of Diamonds were long. Sometimes, when Marm was away, some of the servants would speak to me. I didn't reply. Never again would I engage in human conversation. I was mute and my silence became a dark stone inside me.

Days turned to months and months turned to years. For a talkative bird like myself, silence is a kind of death, but I had made a vow and I was determined to keep it.

One day I realised I was dying. The light had gone out of my eyes and when I looked in the mirror, instead of seeing a bedraggled black macaw, I saw a black hole spiralling into space, an image from one of my least favourite cards – The Abyss. I leaned into my future and felt myself being drawn into the swirling vortex and I'm sure I would have died, had I not heard a voice.

'Oh, you poor creature.'

The kindness in that voice made me forget myself. I broke my vow of silence and was saved.

'My name's Metropolis.' I hardly recognised my voice. It was hoarse and scratchy from years of disuse.

The young maid got such a shock that she dropped her polishing cloth.

'You speak!' she cried.

'I'm the watchbird.'

'Do you work for the mistress?'

'No. I'm a prisoner like you.'

The girl told me she had arrived the night before. She was about to say more when Mistress Adamantine appeared at the top of the stairs.

'I'm going out and I want the Firmament sparkling clean by the time I return.' She pointed to the ladder, a rickety thing that was propped against the wall. 'Get to work, girl!' she ordered. Then she swept down the stairs and left the house.

The Firmament was Marm's name for the stars she'd set in the domed roof of the entrance hall. There were whole constellations of diamonds up there and she liked to see them sparkling.

The maid looked up the ladder and gulped. The ceiling arched high above.

'Take a deep breath,' I told her. I had experience with heights and could advise the girl how to contain her fear so that her trembling did not upset the ladder.

'Look up,' I said. 'Feel the wind under your wings.'

'I can't do it,' she whispered.

'You can. You're strong and fearless.'

I was lying, of course. She was pale as death and weak as a sparrow, and even if she reached the top, it was more than likely that Marm would kick the wobbly ladder out from under her in passing as she had done with the last girl.

I watched her climb. Up she went, hand over hand, rung by rung, until she disappeared into the lofty reaches overhead.

She was up the ladder all day, and although she hadn't finished the job by the time Marm returned, the mistress seemed to have forgotten about her. Marm went straight to the tower and I could hear her muttering to her red stone. When it was dark the maid crept down the ladder.

'Thank you,' she whispered, as she stepped off the bottom rung.

'What's your name?' I asked.

'May.'

She gave me a tiny smile, and from that day on we were friends. Although I never spoke publicly, I spoke to May every day in private, encouraging her, telling her she would not fall. In short, I took her under my wing. One day I even gave her one of my tail feathers, telling her it would bring her luck.

May had been at the House of Diamonds for several weeks before she noticed my cards.

'What are those pictures on the floor of your cage, Metropolis?'

'They're the cards that taught me to speak,' I told her. 'They contain everything there is to know — the past, the present, the future and every possible situation a person could find themselves in.'

She peered into the cage.

'Can you pick one for me?' she asked. 'I want to know my future.'

Her future was as plain as the beak on my face. She would go the same way the last girl had gone, just as I would most likely follow the fate of the last watchbird.

∞∞∞∞∞∞∞∞∞∞∞∞∞∞∞∞∞∞∞∞∞∞∞∞∞∞∞∞∞∞∞∞∞∞∞∞∞∞∞∞∞∞∞∞∞∞∞∞∞∞

'YOU'RE IN THE WRONG CARRIAGE, LAD,' the conductor said. 'This is a first-class ticket. You should be up the front in a sleeper.'

Shoestring made his way to the front of the train. He had a compartment all to himself. The bed had crisp white sheets and there was a notice on the door informing him that breakfast would be served at seven-thirty.

He lay down on the bed and caught his breath. He'd run from the camp and the gloves had pointed the way to the railway station. It was on the other side of town and he couldn't believe how fast he'd moved. He'd run like a champion athlete and arrived just as the last train was leaving. There was no time to buy a ticket. It didn't matter. When the conductor came Shoe handed one over. The gloves had pinched it for him.

He thought Metropolis would most likely be somewhere in Cadenza and he guessed that was where the train was heading. He checked his ticket and tried to make out the name. It didn't look familiar.

As he fell asleep the gloves slipped from his hands. They opened the door and flew out into the corridor, then moved from compartment to compartment sliding into the pockets of sleeping passengers. They opened purses and wallets. They carefully undid the catch on a necklace and they slipped a ring so gently from a woman's finger that she barely stirred.

Shoestring woke once or twice in the night as the train pulled in and out of stations, but mostly he slept peacefully. When he rose the next morning, the gloves were back on his hands; he opened the blinds and the silver stitching on the seams gleamed in the sunlight.

There was a knock at the door and a waiter, wearing white

gloves that looked much like Shoestring's, came in with a tray of steaming food. Shoe put his hands in his pockets, and was surprised to find they were full. When the waiter left he pulled out a wad of notes, a diamond ring, a set of gold cufflinks and a pearl necklace. In the old days he wouldn't have stolen that much in a week and here he was with an impressive haul after just one night. He supposed he should have felt pleased, but it worried him. He stuffed the things away, hoping the owners had left the train.

When the waiter returned to collect the breakfast tray, Shoe held out the ticket and asked what time the train would arrive.

'Seven this evening,' the man told him. 'It's the end of the line.'

EXCEPT FOR A GUARD WHO STOOD BY THE gate waiting to close up for the night, the station was deserted. Shoestring was the only person to get off the train. He looked about. The railway tracks continued but they were overgrown with weeds. In the distance a single mountain rose from the plains. The sides were steep and the top was covered in clouds.

'Where do the tracks lead?' Shoestring asked the guard.

'Nowhere,' the guard replied. 'They used to go to Mount Adamantine. There was once a mine up there but it's been closed for years.'

*How strange*, Shoe thought. *What would Metropolis be doing here?*

He left the station and walked quickly along the tracks. The sun was setting and he wanted to get wherever he was going before nightfall. There were a few buildings about but most of them looked empty, with thistles and long grass growing around them. There were fields on either side of the railway tracks and when these gave way to woodlands, Shoestring wondered if he would have to sleep in the open. He noticed the gloves were giving out a faint light and, as night fell, the light grew stronger. He held his hands out in front of him and the gloves lit his way. They led him through a tunnel and when he came out the other side he found himself walking uphill.

The going was steep but he didn't tire. He began to run and was surprised at the energy he had. He ran along the railway line until it petered out, then he continued along a narrow path that wound its way up the mountain. He ran with long loping strides and, as the night wore on, he lost all sense of time. He felt he could run forever.

The moon moved across the sky and it was dawn by the time he reached the top of the mountain. He came over a ridge and looked down on a vast plateau. In the distance he could see a settlement. It looked like an old mining town and as he came closer he saw the houses were boarded up. Some had lost their roofs.

He couldn't imagine why Metropolis would be in a place like this.

The track he was on led to a huge hole in the ground.

*This must have been the mine*, he thought as he peered over the edge. A path spiralled around the sides of the pit, disappearing into the darkness below. The mine was so deep Shoe couldn't see the bottom. He'd always had a good head for heights but gazing into those depths almost made him dizzy, so he straightened up and looked ahead. A road skirted the pit and led out of town. Shoe followed it.

The sun was up when he saw a wall ahead, made of stone and topped with broken glass. As he approached, the wall seemed to glitter in the morning light and he realised it was encrusted with precious stones. There was a sign on it and he knew what the bottom line said. When he was a thief he avoided places with that warning.

A pair of wrought-iron gates stood wide open and through them Shoe saw a grand but dilapidated mansion with a tower that reached up into the sky. Two guards stood at the front door, a man and a woman. The woman had big muscles

and was covered in tattoos and the man wore studs in his ear that glinted in the sunlight. Both had diamond knuckledusters on their fists and they cracked their fingers as Shoe approached.

'Come in. You're expected.'

The guards stepped aside and opened the front door, waving Shoestring into what must once have been an impressive entrance hall. An enormous chandelier covered in spiderwebs hung from the domed ceiling, which was painted the colour of the night sky – and although it was dusty, he could see it was studded with sparkling stones.

'Diamonds!' he gasped.

'Most precious of gems.' The voice startled Shoestring. He swung around and saw an old woman brandishing a feather duster. She had long silver hair and she was dripping with jewels.

HOUSE OF DIAMONDS

ENTER AT YOUR OWN RISK

The woman walked past Shoestring and began dusting some objects on a little table at the foot of the staircase. There was a picture in a diamond-studded frame and Shoestring gasped when he realised it was a photo of himself, the one May kept on her mantelpiece in the Luck Palace. The glass was smashed. Next to it was a large object covered with a cloth.

'I once had many servants but now I do all the dusting myself.'

With a flourish the old lady suddenly lifted the cloth and threw it across the room.

'Metropolis!' Shoestring cried.

The macaw sat hunched in her cage, blinking at the light.

A S   Y O U   K N O W ,   I ' V E   N E V E R   B E E N   F O N D
of Shoestring, but believe me I was pleased to see him
that day. I'd never been so pleased to see anyone in my life.
I almost fainted with relief. He was wearing the same white
jacket and cravat that he'd worn at the performance at Cadenza
Towers. They looked a bit bedraggled now. Around his neck
was my mirror, the present May had given him to wish him
well in his new career.

I caught sight of my image in that mirror and gasped.
I was a shadow of my former self. My crest had fallen and my
plumage was limp as a tatty feather duster.

Then my beak fell open with shock, for I noticed Shoestring
wore white gloves, the same gloves that had stolen me away, the
gloves that had taken my voice and locked me up in this tiny
prison of a cage.

SHOESTRING STARED AT METROPOLIS. HE
was about to grab the cage and run when he found his hand
slipping through Marm's arm.

'My name is Mistress Adamantine, but you can call me
Marm,' she said.

Shoe let out a cry as his left hand grasped his right, locking him to the old woman.

'Let me go!'

'In time,' Marm told him. 'First I'll show you around. I don't often have visitors.'

Shoestring looked over his shoulder at Metropolis as he was taken up the spiral staircase that led from the entrance hall to the upper reaches of the House of Diamonds.

'I keep my most valuable stones in the tower,' Marm told him. She took him to a room at the very top that had nothing in it except a table, two chairs and a diamond the size of a cannonball. Shoestring was momentarily blinded by its sparkle. He shielded his eyes with his hand and looked away through a small barred window. In the distance he could see the pit and the abandoned mining town.

'Hello, my shining one.'

The diamond glowed brightly at the sound of the old woman's voice. 'This is my favourite stone,' she said. 'Dazzling, isn't he?'

Shoestring didn't reply.

'Isn't he!' she insisted.

The boy nodded. He forced himself to look at the stone. It was red as fire and he could see flames inside it.

'I call him the Eye of the Dragon. The red diamond is very rare.'

She touched the stone, smiling to herself. 'Not so long ago

123

I almost lost him. My shining one was nearly snatched from under my nose. It would have been the second great loss in my life.' She adjusted her monocle and examined the stone.

*She's mad*, Shoestring thought. *I have to get away.*

'But now we are together again,' the old woman continued. 'And we will never be parted.'

She smiled at the diamond then fixed her eyes on Shoestring. 'You'd know all about theft, wouldn't you? You've lived in a den of thieves and been brought up by criminals.'

Shoe stared, wide-eyed.

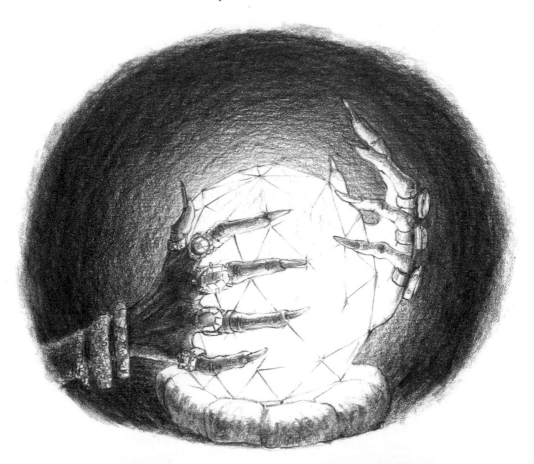

'Oh yes, I know all about you,' she said. 'Your mother – or perhaps you call her aunt – is a felon of the worst order. What a piece of work that woman is. Her crimes are heinous. She's a fiend and a villain. She should be behind bars.'

'That's not true,' Shoestring began. 'May is—'

'I know May. I know what she is!' The woman glowered. Then her voice turned suddenly sweet. 'Let's speak of pleasant things,' she said. 'Tell me, boy, what do you know about diamonds?'

'Not much,' Shoe whispered.

'Speak up. What do you know about diamonds?'

'Nothing.'

'Nothing, MARM.'

'Nothing, Marm.'

*Keep calm*, Shoestring told himself. *Do exactly as she says.*

There was something dangerous about the woman; her grip was unnaturally strong and he didn't want to anger her.

'Well, I'm going to give you a lesson.' She swept her hand towards the little window. 'Look at the sky,' she said. 'Picture this. Once, long ago – a million years ago – a comet was hurtling through space. Do you know what a comet is, boy?' She leaned close to him. 'A shooting star, a flaming ball of fire. Can you see it in your mind's eye?'

Shoestring didn't know what he saw in his mind's eye, but what he saw in front of him was Marm holding up her eyeglass. Behind it, her eyeball was huge, as red and round as a planet. Her pupil reminded Shoe of the dark pit he'd passed on the way here. It was black as night and for a moment he thought he saw something moving in its depths, a tiny comet, trailing flames.

Shoe tried not to look into Marm's terrible eye. He noticed the stone was getting brighter and he stared at that instead.

'The comet crashed to earth and hit with such force that the stones under the ground were turned into precious jewels.' Marm smashed her fist on the table to demonstrate and Shoestring held his breath, rigid with fear.

'The glittering jewels lay deep under the ground for thousands of years and they would have stayed hidden forever, but one day the dragon woke up. What dragon, you ask?'

She paused and stroked the stone as if it was a cat. 'He loves this story,' she said, then she breathed on the diamond and, releasing Shoestring's arm, began polishing it with the hem of her dress.

The moment she let him go Shoe thought of making a run for it. The room was small. He was less than three paces from the door, which she'd left open behind her. He glanced towards it but all at once her face was in front of his, horribly close.

'Look at me when I'm talking to you! Do you know the dragon I mean?'

Shoe was so frightened he could barely speak. 'No,' he said quietly.

'There was a dragon who lived at the centre of the earth. His belly was a forge and his breath was fire. He'd been asleep for a million years. But one day he opened his eyes and roared.

'And when he roared, he spewed out a fire so fierce nothing could withstand it. Rocks were melted and a river of fire surged upwards.'

She stared at Shoestring and he couldn't help looking into her eye. For a moment he saw a volcano inside it. She blinked and it was gone.

'Then the dragon yawned,' she whispered. 'He turned over and went back to sleep. The lava cooled and a single sparkling stone was left lying on the surface. This stone.' Marm picked it up. 'My shining one, my precious wonder. It lay there waiting. Do you know what it was waiting for, my boy?'

Shoestring shook his head. He was trying to decide if he should run now or hold off until a better moment arrived.

'It was waiting for me! I discovered it. I picked it up and knew it was the first of many. That's why this stone is my favourite.'

She held up the diamond with both hands, gazing into it as if it was a crystal ball.

'The Eye of the Dragon has forty-eight faces,' she declared, 'and I see myself in every one of them.'

Shoestring took one look at Marm's face reflected in the faceted diamond, then leapt to his feet and ran. He raced down the spiral stairs to the entrance hall, grabbing Metropolis's cage as he passed. The guards stood aside as he sprinted out the front door, heading for the gates.

In her tower, Marm lowered the huge diamond and took the monocle from her eye. She turned it around and pulled it out into the length of a telescope. There was a series of soft clicks as the lenses adjusted themselves.

'The bait is laid and the trap is set, my dear,' she muttered as she went to the window, following Shoestring's progress as he raced back the way he had come. 'Go, my boy. Run to your precious May and tell her what you've seen.'

Marm turned to the Eye of the Dragon.

'Everything is going according to plan, my shining one,' she whispered.

CHAPTER TWELVE

# HISTORY

'IT WOULDN'T HURT TO THANK ME FOR
rescuing you, Metropolis.'

Shoestring ran past the pit and through the abandoned
town. The bedraggled macaw clutched the bars of the cage
as it bounced up and down and banged against the boy's
leg.

*He could at least be a bit careful*, Metropolis thought. But still,
he'd found her, saved her, stolen her back. She couldn't have
gone on much longer – another week and she would have
fallen from the perch.

'All right, don't answer!' He reached the ridge and headed
down the same track he had come up the night before. 'How
did you come to be with that crazy old woman?'

*How did you come to find me?* Metropolis thought.

'She said she knew May.'

*She knew her all right, and me too*, Metropolis said to herself.
It was so long ago, almost another life. They say your past
catches up with you when you least expect it.

Metropolis's thoughts rattled around inside her head with the motion of the cage. It was hard to keep hold of them. They scattered like the husks of sunflower seeds. Why wouldn't he slow down? You'd think he'd show some consideration.

The track was rocky and small shrubs grew between the stones. Boulders occasionally blocked the way but Shoestring leapt over them and whenever he did, Metropolis lost her grip and was thrown upside down on the floor of the cage.

Shoestring was still full of energy. Whether it was from fear or from the gloves, he didn't know. He raced down the side of the mountain and when he reached the old railway line he ran faster than ever. He looked over his shoulder now and then but nobody was following.

*Strange how the guards let me pass*, he thought. *And it seems Marm hasn't sent them after me.*

He ran through the tunnel and out the other side, and when he reached the station he put the cage on the platform and began scanning the ground.

'Lost something?' the railway guard asked.

Shoestring told him he needed a piece of wire or a hair slide, something to pick the lock of the cage. When the guard produced a paperclip Shoe opened the door and Metropolis hopped out. She was so thin and dishevelled he almost felt sorry for her.

'How did you end up on the mountain?' he asked.

The bird blinked at him and turned her back.

'That'd be right,' he muttered. 'Usually you never shut up and now you won't answer a simple question.'

'Does the next train go anywhere near Cadenza?' he asked the guard. Metropolis looked up. Cadenza! Oh, to be back at the Luck Palace!

'Change at Whybrow Junction,' the guard said.

Shoestring sat down on the platform to wait.

'How long are you going to keep this up, Metropolis?' he asked. 'I saved you, didn't I? Don't give me the silent treatment.'

Metropolis gave him a sharp look. *You little fool*, she thought. Then, exhausted from her ordeal – the weeks, or was it months she spent in the cage, not to mention the rough ride down the mountain – she closed her eyes and went to sleep.

SHE DREAMED OF EVENTS LONG AGO. SHE was back at the House of Diamonds.

'Please pick a card for me,' May asked. 'I need to know what's ahead.'

'There's nothing ahead,' Metropolis replied. 'There's no future.'

But the young girl pleaded and begged until Metropolis did as she asked. The card she picked up and held in her beak was The Rising Star, a surprising image considering the circumstances.

'What does it mean, Metropolis?' May's eyes were full of hope and for a second Metropolis thought there might be hope for her as well. She asked the maid to open the cage.

May's thin face grew thinner. 'Marm would kill me,' she whispered.

'The key's in the drawer.' Metropolis knew this because she'd seen it every time the drawer was opened.

'I'll do it,' May breathed. She put her hand on the knob and pulled out the drawer, but at that moment Marm appeared.

'Why aren't you working?' she called from the top of the stairs.

'I was just looking for a clean cloth,' May stammered.

Marm pointed to the Firmament.

'Get to your task,' she cried. 'And stay there... ALL NIGHT!'

Metropolis dreamed of that long night. She dreamed she was whispering into the dark, hoping her words would rise all the way up to the stars. She knew how terrified May would be alone up there and tried to comfort her.

'Hold tight. Think of the card,' she said. 'The Rising Star is bright and beautiful. It will light your way all through the night.'

When Metropolis stopped talking she heard a scratching sound in the hollow reaches above and wondered if May was trying to get a grip on one of the diamonds. Then there were footsteps and the scratching stopped. She heard a clinking of keys and from the corner of her eye saw Jack Diamond creeping into the entrance hall. He was holding a small case of the type that Marm used for carrying her precious stones when she went away on trading trips. He set the case on the floor and when he opened it his face shone in the light of the diamonds packed inside. He took a screwdriver from his back pocket, then looked up and made a whistling sound between his teeth.

'Too high,' he muttered. 'The brightest stars are out of reach. But I'll help myself to the lower constellations.'

He stood on tiptoes and began gouging a diamond from the wall.

'That's the beauty of the plaster setting – the diamonds are easily prised out.'

Metropolis kept perfectly still, hoping the man wouldn't remember she was there. But when he dropped the stone into his case he noticed her.

'Ah, the watchbird!' he breathed, putting a finger to his lips. He moved towards the table and, opening the drawer, took out the key.

Petrified, Metropolis watched him open her cage. When he reached towards her, she knew he intended to wring her neck.

METROPOLIS WOKE WITH A START. SHE was appalled to find herself in Shoestring's arms. She gave him a sharp peck on the wrist and he dropped her immediately, not onto the platform at the station but onto a pavement. Metropolis looked up and saw houses, shopfronts and a familiar-looking bakery. She opened her beak and let out a silent squawk. She was on Viva Street. She was home! She was only a block away from the Luck Palace. She tried to take to the air but found she was so weak she could barely stand up, let alone fly.

'Now you're awake you can sit on my shoulder,' Shoestring said. 'Promise you won't peck?'

Metropolis nodded. She had no choice.

When Shoestring was in sight of the Luck Palace he paused and looked at his hands. *I'd better put these gloves away*, he told himself. *They've done their work.*

The gloves had slipped on easily but he had trouble getting them off. They seemed to cling to him, and he had to ask a passer-by for help. Once one was off, he could use his free hand to take off the other.

Suddenly he felt exhausted – so tired he doubted he could walk the last few steps of the way. Metropolis had fallen asleep again and although she wasn't half the bird she used to be, to him she was a dead weight. He couldn't remember ever feeling so tired. But then he'd never run up and down a mountain before. He put the gloves in his jacket pocket, and walked wearily to the door of Mr Goldfiend's shop.

❦

WHEN METROPOLIS NEXT WOKE SHE FOUND herself sitting on a cushion on the chaise longue in the gaming room. Her own china water bowl was in front of her and she saw it was full of grape juice. Parched, she took a beakful. There were cries of relief from May, Ruby and Mr Goldfiend.

'Don't speak, darl,' May said. 'Don't say a word. You have to get your strength back.' She turned to Shoestring. 'Why didn't you bring her home sooner, love? She looks so ill. She must have caught something. Where's Ace and the others? Didn't they come with you?'

'Metropolis wasn't with the troupe, May,' Shoestring sighed. 'I had to go and find her.'

*That's right, just speak over me as if I'm not here,* Metropolis thought. She tried to lift one wing.

'Well, where was she?' May asked.

Ruby put another bowl on the cushion. 'I've made fruit salad. It's your favourite, Metropolis – figs and fresh berries.'

Metropolis blinked as May offered her a strawberry on the end of a silver spoon. She ate it and looked up.

'Where was she?' May asked again.

Shoestring was almost too tired to speak. 'I don't know, some place on top of a mountain.'

'What mountain?'

'It was an odd place. Some sort of mining town.'

May and Ruby exchanged worried glances.

'What was the name of the mountain?' May wanted to know.

Shoestring yawned. He could barely keep his eyes open. 'Mount Adamantine.'

It was shock that made May faint. She felt suddenly cold and the blood rushed from her head. In that dizzy state the voices of the people around her faded. She gasped and took a sharp breath and the sound seemed to whistle in her ears like a mountain wind. She was fourteen again, cold and hungry and dressed in rags. The wind grew stronger. It was night and she'd been walking for hours, or was it days? When she saw lights in the distance she knew she'd reached a settlement.

*I'm saved*, she thought.

She went to the first house and knocked. A dog barked and a worried-looking woman opened the door a crack.

'What do you want?' she whispered.

May could barely speak. 'Please … a crust of bread …'

The woman pointed to a sign that was swinging in the wind: *NO BEGGARS, HAWKERS OR PEDLARS. BY ORDER M. A.*

'If you want work go and ask at the mine.' She closed the door.

May trudged down the street. She hadn't eaten for days
and when she came to the pit she thought she was dreaming.
She looked over the edge. The place was lit with a circle
of burning lamps and she saw thousands of workers filing
along a path that spiralled around the sides of the crater. They
were carrying baskets of earth on their heads and they looked
worse off than she was, if that was possible. A man on the path
below was yelling, 'Get a move on!' He looked up and saw
her staring.

'What are you after?' he cried. 'Are you looking for work?'

May nodded, although she was so weak she could hardly
stand.

'Go and ask the mistress.' He pointed away from the pit.

Snow crunched underfoot. May had no shoes and her feet were bound in rags. She left the mine and walked beyond the town. Before long she found herself standing before the gates of a grand house. ᴇɴᴛᴇʀ ᴀᴛ ʏᴏᴜʀ ᴏᴡɴ ʀɪsᴋ, the sign said. She felt she didn't have much choice.

'You're thin and scrawny,' the mistress muttered, 'but I'll give you a try. Tomorrow you'll start polishing my collection.'

The woman called for her servants. 'Take this wretched girl to the kitchen and give her something to eat.'

Soon May was sitting in a cold kitchen eating a tiny bowl of food. The maids were with her.

'It's not much, but it's better than nothing,' said the girl next to her. 'Here, have some of mine.' She scraped two teaspoons of food into May's bowl. 'My name is Ruby.'

'Thank you,' May whispered. 'I couldn't have gone any further.'

'But you should have. It's easy to enter the House of Diamonds but hard to leave.'

'Be careful of Marm,' another maid whispered. 'She's got a diamond where her heart should be.'

'She's cold and cruel,' Ruby said quietly.

The girls nodded. They all looked thin and scared.

'Her son is worse,' said a girl on the other side of the table. 'His name is Jack Diamond.'

After May had eaten they took her to the maids' room, which was no more than a prison cell.

'Don't you have beds or blankets?' May asked.

'Marm won't give us any. She wants us to sleep on the cold floor.'

'But it's stone and it's the middle of winter.'

Ruby sighed. 'Everything here is stone,' she said.

Each girl had a thin straw mattress and a tiny rug. There were no spares for May.

'Try and sleep. You'll need your strength for the morning,' Ruby told her. 'The new girl always gets the worst job.'

'What job's that?' May asked, as she lay down.

'Polishing the Firmament,' one of the maids answered. 'You'll be up the ladder cleaning the stars.'

'But I'm afraid of heights.'

'So was the last girl,' Ruby whispered.

MR GOLDFIEND HELD OUT A CUP OF TEA and looked at May with concern.

'She's coming round,' said Ruby.

They helped May sit up and slowly she sipped her tea. She was pale and her hands were shaking so much she spilled some in the saucer. She took a deep breath and tried to collect herself.

'Shoestring, did you meet anyone on that mountain?' she asked.

'A lady with a monocle. Her name was Marm. She said she knew you.'

A look of dread passed over May's face and she shuddered.

'What's wrong, May?' Mr Goldfiend cried. 'You look like you've seen a ghost.'

'Not a ghost, Edwin,' May muttered under her breath. She tried to steady her hands. 'Thank goodness you're safe, Shoe. You'll stay here with me.'

Shoe thought of the troupe. Maybe they had stayed where they were, waiting for him, or perhaps they were already on their way to Cadenza. Now that Metropolis was found there was no need for them to come.

'I have to go back and join the others,' he said. 'They'll be wondering where I am.'

'No, no!' May was alarmed. 'You must stay here. I'm not having you leave the Luck Palace.'

Shoestring gave May a puzzled look. She'd always let him do whatever he liked; that was the beauty of her. 'But my act, the troupe ... We're on our way to a festival, or we were until Metropolis got lost. I'm in a competition.'

'Let's talk about it in the morning,' Ruby suggested. 'You need to go to bed.' She led Shoestring to his old room on the top floor.

As soon as they left the gaming room, May turned to Metropolis.

'I didn't think she'd still be alive.'

Metropolis nodded.

'Who?' Mr Goldfiend asked. 'What's this all about, May?'

'History, Mr Goldfiend. It's about someone we used to know, a diamond trader called Mistress Adamantine.' May put down her cup and saucer. 'You've got contacts. Would you ask around and see what you can find out about her?'

Mr Goldfiend hurried away and May lifted Metropolis onto her lap.

'Tell me what happened, darl,' she said. 'Start at the beginning.'

Metropolis shook her head.

'Surely you're not sulking?' May cried.

Metropolis looked deep into May's eyes, trying to make her understand. There was so much she wanted to say. She wanted to tell May how terrible it was to be in that cage again, how she was lucky not to have died. She wanted to explain what a tragedy it was for a Fabulous Macaw to look as she did now, scrawny and bedraggled. And she wished she could tell May that the biggest tragedy of all was the loss of her voice. To steal away her words was a cruel and vicious crime. She was a bird full of opinions and to be rendered mute was agony. She opened her beak but the only sound she could make was a dry rattle, like wind blowing through seed heads beside an abandoned railway line.

# CHAPTER THIRTEEN

# DEAR MAY

SHOESTRING FELL ASLEEP AS SOON AS HIS head hit the pillow. He'd been too tired to take off his trousers. He slung his jacket over the chair next to the bed, said goodnight to Ruby and knew nothing for several hours. He didn't see the wrinkles in his jacket change as the gloves made their way out of his pocket. He didn't hear them strike a match and light the bedside lamp. He woke when he felt someone shaking him by the shoulders. Then he looked up and saw the shadow on the wall.

'Get up. It's time to go.'

'Go?' Shoestring rubbed his eyes. 'Go where?'

'You want to go back to the troupe, don't you? I'll show you the way.'

'Who *are* you?' Shoe demanded.

There was a soft, breathy laugh. 'I'm a pair of willing hands. I helped you find Metropolis and I'll help you find whatever your heart desires. Up you get!'

Shoestring felt himself being dragged by the ear.

Dear May,
Sorry I had to leave without saying goodbye. I love my life in the troupe and I must go back to it. Don't worry about me I'm in safe hands
Love,
Shoestring xx
p.s. Don't follow me

'I can't leave without saying goodbye to May,' he began.
'No problem. I'll write her a note.'

PART THREE

# CHAPTER FOURTEEN

# A Poor Show

SHOESTRING ARRIVED BACK AT THE
campsite in the middle of the night. Just what night, he wasn't
sure. He had been travelling for days. He slipped into the tent
and woke his friend.

'Kid, I'm back!'

KidGlovz did not look pleased to see him.

'Where have you been? Lovegrove and Ace have been
worried sick.'

'I went looking for Metropolis and I found her. Those
gloves, Kid – they showed me the way.'

'You promised to get rid of them.'

'I know, but without them I would never have rescued
Metropolis.' He pulled the gloves from his pocket, and the wad
of notes and the necklace fell out. Kid peered at them in the
dim light that came from the gloves.

'I thought you'd given up being a thief.'

'I have. I had.'

'And now you're a liar as well?' Kid noticed that Shoestring looked ragged. His face was scratched and the cuffs of his jacket were frayed.

'Throw those gloves away, Shoe. Please.'

Shoestring sighed. He regretted slinking away in the night without telling May. And he didn't like the way the gloves had pulled him by the ear, or the way they had spoken to him, but he remembered the rush of energy when he ran up the mountain. It was a marvellous feeling.

Kid looked at him, pleading.

'All right,' Shoe said. 'I'll get rid of them.'

He left the tent and walked towards the river, but then hesitated. It seemed a waste to throw the gloves away. He went some distance along the riverbank in case KidGlovz was watching, then he skirted back to the camp. He needed time to think.

There was a bag outside Grimwade's tent that was used to store tent pegs. Shoe put the gloves in the bag and pulled the drawstring tight. Then, without making a sound, he crept to the wagon and, being careful not to wake Ace, reached under the ends of the shafts and put the bag in a niche above the axle.

'They're gone,' he told KidGlovz when he returned to the tent. 'I'm sorry, Kid.'

Shoestring felt a small stab of guilt, but what else could he do? The gloves were too precious to throw away.

EVERYONE WAS UPSET THE NEXT MORNING.

'We didn't know what had happened to you,' the Dittos cried. 'We were worried.'

'We've been waiting for days. Where are the gloves?' Lovegrove asked.

Shoestring shot Kid an accusing glance.

'I haven't got them.' He turned out his pockets to prove it. 'I threw them away.'

Sylvie looked closely at Shoestring. She thought of him as her big brother, but there was something different about him that morning.

'I needed to find Metropolis.' Shoestring scanned the faces of his friends. 'For May,' he added.

'You ran off without telling anyone where you were going,' Lovegrove said.

'I didn't know,' Shoestring replied. 'I'm sorry, Lovegrove. I didn't mean any harm. Let's start practising.'

The troupe dispersed and the morning's rehearsal began. Nobody was satisfied with Shoestring's explanation.

Shoe was about to tie his rope to a tree when he felt a tap on his shoulder.

'Oh, it's you!'

One of the gloves put a finger to his lips, then they both gave him a wave and disappeared into a nearby tree.

A short while later a cry went up from Violet. 'No, Daisy. It's an apple! Weren't you listening?'

'You sent me the wrong message,' Daisy said. 'Let's try it again.'

Shoestring watched the girls. Daisy was blindfolded and facing the other way. Violet held an apple on the palm of her hand.

Faster than thought the gloves swooped down from the tree and switched the apple for a pear. They gave Shoe another wave and then they ducked behind the tree.

'It's an apple,' said Violet. She lifted her blindfold and turned around. 'What are you playing at, Daisy? Stop that!'

Shoestring put down his rope and clapped. He wasn't applauding the twins. He put his hands together for the gloves. He could see what they were doing – everyone was angry with him so they were trying to cheer him up. There was no harm in that.

The twins scowled at him.

'Let's go and practise somewhere else,' Daisy said. She turned and walked away, but Violet didn't follow.

'You can go, I'm staying here!' Violet didn't move her mouth, but Shoestring heard her as if she'd spoken aloud. He stared in surprise and she stared back.

'What's he up to?' she asked herself, or maybe she was asking Daisy. Shoe heard her thoughts but it was obvious that Daisy didn't. The other girl didn't turn around. Shoestring shrugged.

He wandered over to Ace, who gave him a nod and fanned out his cards in a showy way.

'Pick a card, any card,' he said, holding them out. 'Look at it then give it back. Don't tell me what it is.' He gave Shoe a wink.

*Ace, at least, isn't holding a grudge,* Shoe thought as he glanced at the card. It was the joker. He handed it back to his uncle.

Shoestring knew how Ace did his trick. He would palm the card while pretending to put it back in the pack, then he'd slip it away somewhere before scratching his head as if he couldn't for the life of him think where that card might be.

Ace gave a confident smile. He loved the cards and the trick never failed. 'I think it's the joker,' he said. 'And I wouldn't be surprised if it was...'

Shoe couldn't help laughing when the gloves swiped the card. He felt them slip it into his back pocket. Ace got such a shock when the card wasn't under his collar that he dropped the rest of the pack.

'Let me try.' Shoestring picked the cards up off the ground.

He flourished and fanned and riffled in a way he'd never learned to do. Then he split the deck and did a slow-motion cascading shuffle with an ease that suggested he'd been practising all his life.

*Just like a pro,* Ace thought. *How can that be?*

Shoestring was so impressed by the way the cards moved for him that he didn't notice his uncle put his head in his hands.

'I don't understand it,' Ace muttered. 'The boy's an expert and I'm losing my touch.'

There was rustling in the tree above Shoestring's head and when he looked up the gloves were hanging from a bough. They pointed towards Grimwade, who had two drumsticks in one hand and a wooden spoon in the other, with which he was tapping the cymbal. *Tock-a-tock crash. Tock-a-tock crash.*

Shoe hurried in that direction, skipping in time to the beat. Drumming was a skill he would enjoy! He could already feel the rhythm in his hands and he was disappointed when Lovegrove called that it was time for the troupe to pack up.

*Later!* he thought. Those gloves had definitely lifted his spirits. He felt strangely pleased with himself.

But nobody else was. He looked at the frowning faces around him and was suddenly confused. What had come over him? These were his friends and he'd upset them, or the gloves had.

After that, he made an effort to be helpful. He took down Lovegrove's tent as well as his own and he put the cooking gear away for Grimwade. He groomed Haul and hitched him to the wagon, a job Ace normally did, then he offered to help Sylvie with her suitcase. But everyone remained in a bad mood with him; they barely thanked him for his help.

Shoestring had no idea what had happened to the gloves. He hoped he'd seen the last of them. As he climbed into the back of the wagon he took the joker card from his pocket.

'Where did you get that?' Ace asked.

Shoe didn't know how to answer. He shrugged and looked at the floor and his face was hot with shame.

When they arrived in the next town, Shoestring did more than his share in setting up for the show. Lovegrove watched him work. She hadn't been convinced by his explanation and later, while he was helping Grimwade sell tickets for the show, she had a quiet word to Lobe.

'I don't like to ask you to eavesdrop on the troupe, but can you keep your ears open as far as Shoestring is concerned? I don't think he's telling us everything.'

THAT NIGHT THE TROUPE OF MARVELS didn't perform well. Sylvie played off-key and Ace was hissed out of the ring. The Dittos' mind-reading act failed miserably and when they danced they were out of step. KidGlovz's music sounded terrible and he couldn't understand why. He'd never played badly before. But Shoestring knew. He'd seen one of the gloves wriggle under the keyboard before Kid went on and he'd seen the other slip out from between the bellows after he'd finished. He'd watched them opening Sylvie's violin case before the show and twisting the tuning pegs. When he'd tried to stop them they had grabbed hold of him and flung him away.

153

'That girl can't play to save herself,' someone in the audience had shouted. There was very little applause, except for Shoestring. The crowd roared, both with relief after having sat through such a poor show and with wonder at the last marvellous act. Shoestring's performance was as brilliant as ever. 'Stunning!' the audience cried. They couldn't believe what they saw.

Afterwards, the troupe sat around the fire and tried to understand what had happened.

Sylvie ran her fingers along the strings of her violin. 'I don't know why I was out of tune,' she said. 'Maybe the strings are losing tension. Either that, or the pegs slipped.'

Hugo sat with his head on KidGlovz's lap. He was out of sorts. He'd refused to accompany Lovegrove when she opened the show, preferring to sit behind the tent with his paws over his nose, and now he looked at Kid with large sorrowful eyes and gave the occasional whimper.

'I don't know what's wrong with him,' Kid said. 'I guess we all had a bad night. Not every show can be perfect.'

*I was perfect*, Shoestring thought. He should have felt pleased, but he didn't. He resolved to find the gloves and get rid of them. He should have done that in the first place. Once they were gone he'd tell his friends what had happened.

There was no singing by the campfire that evening. Ace packed away his cards and went to bed straight after dinner; the others were not far behind him.

Lobe lay in his hammock listening to the sounds of the camp. His daughters were arguing in the wagon.

'You ruined our act, Violet.'

'I did not!'

'We usually always agree,' Daisy muttered.

'No, we don't.'

'Are you awake, Shoe?' Lobe heard KidGlovz whisper in his tent. 'I can't understand why the show went so badly. Are you sure you got rid of those gloves?'

Shoe stood up. 'I'm sorry, Kid.'

'Hey! Where are you going?' Kid asked.

'For a walk.'

'At this hour?'

'I won't be long.'

Shoe searched the campsite. He looked under the wagon in case the gloves had gone back in the tent-peg bag but they weren't there. He scanned the surrounding trees but there was no sign of them. He looked under Grimwade's cooking pots and in Haul's feedbin. He searched every place he could think of and finally he threw up his hands in despair. The moment he did that, the gloves slipped on. Shoe tried to resist but the gloves felt snug and warm and they made his fingers tingle. He tried to remember that the gloves had ruined every act but his – it didn't seem to matter. He flexed his wrists as the energy surged up his arms into his body. Then he grinned and looked around.

Lobe was lying in his hammock with his arms behind his neck. He cocked his head and then threw his legs over one side and stepped out, looking into the dark and listening. Shoe kept perfectly still until Lobe sat down on a box next to the wagon, then he tiptoed away from the campsite.

He hadn't gone far when he saw a cat out on the night's prowl. The cat paused to look at him, one paw raised.

The gloves moved faster than thought and the cat hissed and spat. Shoe smiled to himself and padded silently through the night. When he heard an owl he looked up into the trees. *If I had those eyes I could see in the dark*, he thought. Again the gloves left his hands. In less than a few seconds Shoe saw the world as never before. His night vision was extraordinary. He hurried back to the campsite, where he spotted Lobe.

EARLY THE NEXT MORNING THE DITTO
girls began work on a new pose.

'I'll be the front legs and you be the back,' Violet told her
sister as she moved from a handstand into a backbend.

'I want to be the front,' Daisy insisted.

The pose wasn't going smoothly.

'Dad, how does this look?' they called.

Lobe and Shoestring were strapping tent poles to the top
of the wagon. Lobe took no notice of the girls until they
yelled at him.

'Lobe, does this look like a grasshopper or not?'

Lobe turned around, puzzled. He could barely hear what
they were saying.

# CHAPTER FIFTEEN

# THE SLEEP THIEF

IT HAD BEEN A WHILE SINCE SHOESTRING flew the coop and I was in the third stage of my recovery. My breast feathers had grown back and my plumage had regained much of its former lustre. My weight was almost back to normal thanks to Ruby, who'd instructed Cookie to prepare a special menu, and my eyes were bright again. I was beginning to feel my old self when May received a letter from Ace.

I looked over her shoulder as she read it.

Dearest May,

I got trouble with the boy. He's out all night and won't say where he's been. He never seems to sleep and since he's gone off the rails all our acts are failing. Lobe's lost his hearing and the Dittos are arguing day and night. Little Sylvie's violin won't stay in tune and KidGlovz's accordion sounds like something in pain. The only act that's any good is Shoestring's. I need your help. The boy loves you more than anyone in the world. He needs to show his hand. You'll get an answer out of him. Please come as soon as you can. We'll wait here until you arrive.

With love
Your Ace – ~~King of the Cards~~

PS I got to warn you, May – Shoe is not the boy you once knew.

**The letter almost made me have a relapse. My crest drooped and I felt queasy in my crop. Ace had sent it from some far-flung town that I'd never heard of. He'd written the directions on the back of the envelope.**

**'We'll leave at once,' May said.**

**I watched her bustle about the room. She was in a flap – I could tell by the way she was throwing things into our suitcases.**

'I feel sick,' I told her. 'I'm not well enough to travel.'

'You only think about yourself, Metropolis. That's your trouble.'

May snapped the suitcase shut and without another word she tucked me under her arm and headed out the door.

〰〰〰〰〰〰〰〰〰〰〰〰〰〰〰〰〰〰〰〰〰〰〰〰〰〰〰〰〰〰〰〰〰〰〰

THE TROUPE WAITED FOR MAY. THERE WAS a show every night but it only had one act: Shoestring – The Boy Who Walks on Air. There was no point in the rest of them performing. They practised in the daytime as usual but their confidence was shaken and they didn't dare go into the ring. At night they couldn't sleep.

'First he doesn't rest for weeks and now he's snoring his head off.' Ace looked towards Shoestring's tent as he shuffled the cards.

'And we're all wide awake.' Lovegrove took the hand Ace dealt her. 'What's the time, Mr Grimwade?' she asked.

Grimwade pulled out his fob watch. 'Two o'clock.'

'I think he's stolen our sleep,' Sylvie decided.

Lovegrove groaned. She hadn't had a wink of sleep for days and she was irritable. 'Don't be silly, Sylvie. Sleep can't be stolen.'

'Why not?' Lobe asked from beneath his droopy eyelids. 'There's probably no end to what he can steal. He's taken most of my hearing.'

'You don't know that, Lobe.' Ace frowned at his cards. He'd dealt himself a poor hand.

'Well, it's missing,' Lobe told him. 'And so are a lot of other things.'

'I've lost a cooking pot and I can't find my favourite recipe,' Grimwade yawned.

'Where do you keep your recipes, Mr Grimwade?' Sylvie asked.

'In my head.'

Sylvie turned to the Dittos. 'Have you girls lost anything?'

'My earrings,' Violet said. 'Daisy stole them.'

'I did not!' her sister cried.

Lobe shook his head. 'My girls have lost their harmony. They used to get on well and now they hate each other.'

'That's true,' Violet said. 'I can't stand her.'

'Has anyone else lost anything?' Lovegrove asked.

Hugo whined and sniffed the air, smelling nothing. Sylvie thought of her violin that had once kept perfect pitch. She'd also lost some notes from the concerto Kid had written for her.

'What about you, Kid?' Lovegrove asked.

KidGlovz stroked Hugo's ears. 'I've lost my best friend,' he said, sadly. 'I don't trust Shoestring anymore.'

# CHAPTER SIXTEEN

# Big Night Tonight

I THOUGHT IT WAS A RIDICULOUS IDEA, LEAVING
the Luck Palace. I should have dug in my claws. I'd had
enough of adventuring and this was a wild goose chase if ever
I saw one. But what could I say? I was mute as a stuffed parrot.
I sat on May's shoulder and stared out the train window
as the countryside slipped by, and when she offered me

titbits from the packet she kept in her
handbag — sunflower seeds and glazed
cherries — I refused to eat in order to
punish her.

We arrived at our destination at
night. The show was on and we could
hear the applause as soon as we stepped
off the train. It seemed that everybody
in the town was at the performance,
everybody except the troupe.

Grimwade stood glumly at the entrance to the main tent and the others were sitting at a campsite behind it. Ace was shuffling cards in a distracted fashion. The twins were bickering and the boy, KidGlovz, sat with his head in his hands. When they saw us, they brightened and Madame Lovegrove ran to greet May.

'Thank goodness you've arrived!' she cried. She began telling May what had been happening. The others joined in and soon everyone was talking at once.

May sat on her suitcase and listened. You could see she didn't know what to make of it, but to me it was perfectly clear – the boy had fouled his own nest and the troupe had turned against him.

'Why are you blaming Shoestring?' May asked. 'Things have gone wrong but it might not be his fault.'

'Everything was fine until he went off to find the bird,' KidGlovz told her. 'Since then things have gone from bad to worse.'

'Once a thief always a thief,' Lobe said.

'But he gave all that up.' May didn't want to believe bad things about her boy. 'And what you're accusing him of stealing…well, it doesn't add up.'

'I'm sure it's the gloves,' Kid said. 'They're to blame, not him.'

'What gloves are you talking about?' May asked.

'These gloves.'

**When Daisy opened the book and pointed to the picture, my crest shot up and I let out a silent scream.**

✧◇◇◇◇◇◇◇◇◇◇◇◇◇◇◇◇◇◇◇◇◇◇◇◇◇◇◇◇◇◇◇◇◇◇◇◇◇◇◇◇◇◇◇✧

LOVEGROVE LOOKED OVER DAISY'S SHOULDER and frowned. 'Those were the gloves that Kid once owned. They made him into a master musician but they nearly ruined his life.'

'They got out of control,' Kid said.

May tried to take it in. Shoe had dreamed about some gloves; that's what he'd been talking about on the night of the raid. She turned to Lovegrove. 'All this is making my head ache,' she said. 'It's time for me to lay my cards on the table. I don't know anything about these gloves but I think Shoestring is being used. I have an enemy – someone Metropolis and I used to know many years ago – and I think she's involved.'

May was about to go on when a roar of applause rose from the tent. The show was over and the crowd began pouring out. People milled around, hoping to catch a glimpse of The Boy Who Walks on Air to see what he looked like when he was on the ground. They wanted to touch the invisible rope and ask him how he did the impossible, so it was some time before Shoestring knew May was there.

When he saw her he let out a whoop of joy and ran to her. She noticed the mirror she'd given him was dangling around his neck. She held out her arms to him.

'Are you all right, Shoe?' she asked as she hugged him.

'I'm better than all right!' Shoestring stepped back and grinned. 'The crowds love me. And look what came today – my entry card to the Festival of Marvels!' He took a card from his top pocket and proudly handed it to May.

CONGRATULATIONS ON BEING CHOSEN TO COMPETE IN THE DEATH-DEFYING FAME AND FORTUNE AWARD FOR THE WORLD'S LEADING HIGHWIRE ARTIST. PRESENT THIS CARD ON ARRIVAL AND PROCEED TO THE COMPETITORS' STAND. PLEASE BE ADVISED THAT THE JUDGE'S DECISION IS FINAL AND NO CORRESPONDENCE WILL BE ENTERED INTO.

'I'll win!' he told her. 'Will you come and watch me?' He took out his invitation and studied the map on the back. 'We can go there together.'

'Shoe, your friends aren't happy,' May said. 'They're worried about you and so am I.'

Shoestring didn't look up from the map. 'There's nothing to worry about.'

'What's this business about the gloves?'

'What gloves?' He hated to lie to May but what else could he do?

'When you left the Luck Palace there was a note on your beside table. Who wrote it?'

'Nobody.'

'Please tell the truth.' May gave Shoestring a steady look. 'I've cared for you since you were a baby, Shoe. Your father had nothing left to lose so he put you on the table, and I reckoned a man like that didn't deserve to have a child. I looked for your mother and learned she had died so I brought you up as my own. I watched you grow into the best thief in Cadenza and I was proud of you. Then, when you became a performer, I was even more proud because I didn't have to worry that one day you would get caught. I liked the fact that you were earning an honest living – something that I'd never done. But now I fear for you.'

Shoestring looked towards the tent.

'I've got to go, May. I've got to put my rope away.'

'Sit down,' she said sternly. 'I'm going to tell you a story, a true story. There are things in my past I'd rather forget, but they seem to have come back to haunt me.'

Shoestring glanced at Metropolis in alarm when May took out her cards. He thought she was going to ask the bird to read them and reveal what had happened. He hoped Metropolis hadn't found her voice. He was relieved when May didn't lay out a spread. Instead, she flipped through the pack until she found The Rising Star.

'I was a young girl when I stumbled into the House of Diamonds,' she began. 'I was cold and hungry and I was looking for a job.'

The troupe listened as May recounted her story. She told of her first meeting with Mistress Adamantine and how she was given the dangerous task of polishing the diamonds that were set into the ceiling. When she described how she stood on the top rung of the wobbly ladder and reached up, Sylvie gasped.

'I used my fingernails to prise out a stone,' May said. 'I nearly lost my balance.'

Shoestring was only half listening. His mind was full of the gloves and, if some of the troupe closed their eyes and imagined young May teetering on top of the ladder, he saw a different picture: a shadow on the wall, the silhouette of a person with a hooked nose and small goatee beard. He saw it in his mind and he heard the shadow speak.

'Big night tonight. Are you ready?'

Shoestring was dimly aware of May ending her story – something about how she ran through the night with Metropolis on her shoulder.

'Ready for what?' He wasn't sure if he asked the question aloud.

'The main event. The big show. Everything else has just been a dress rehearsal.' The voice echoed through Shoestring's head.

'Shoestring? Shoe!' Someone was calling him.

Shoestring blinked and stared into May's face. Had he been daydreaming?

'Tell me the truth about those gloves,' she demanded.

'There's nothing to tell, May,' he muttered, doubtfully.

May sighed. 'Are you sure?'

Shoestring wasn't sure of anything.

'We'll sleep now,' May told him. 'We can talk again in the morning.' He was glad she was taking charge. 'Promise me you won't go running off tonight?

'All right,' he said. 'I promise.'

MADAME LOVEGROVE HAD GRIMWADE put up a spare tent for May and me, and although I was used to more luxurious surroundings I decided the accommodation was adequate. I was weary from our journey and wouldn't have complained even if I had to sleep in a tree. But as it turned out, I wasn't to sleep that night.

'Watch him, Metropolis,' May said, after the boys went to bed. 'Watch him until morning. Don't take your eagle eyes off him.'

What did she think I was – the *watchbird*?

'Please, Metropolis.' She gave me a pleading look.

The dog – that wolfhound I'd seen at Cadenza Towers – was lying outside the boys' tent door as if he was on guard. I gave him a wide berth and hopped under the tent flap, then I skirted the sleeping boys and hid myself behind an accordion. I had no idea what I would do if anything happened; I'd have to wing it.

An hour or so passed, then someone struck a match.

If I had a voice I would have squawked – the gloves were in the tent! They lit a candle and then they clasped each other. They were fat and white and full of themselves. They might have been the severed hands of a conjurer who was about to release a giant white rabbit or some other terrible creature. I looked past them to the wavering shadow they were making on the canvas. At first I thought it was a goat … then I saw it was a man, the same man I had seen on the wall of the wagon the night I followed the troupe all the way from Cadenza. And the voice was the same, soft and full of shadows.

'Good evening, my friend.'

'Not tonight.' Shoestring sat up. 'I can't tonight. I promised May …'

'Come, come.' The shadow sounded annoyed. 'We have work to do. Hold out your hands.'

Shoestring clasped the mirror and held it to his chest as if it was a little shield that he hoped would protect him. When he did this, the gloves moved closer to the candle and the shadow grew until it covered the whole wall of the tent.

I'm a tough old bird and I've seen more fights at the Luck Palace than you can imagine, but I didn't like the look of where this one was heading. I cringed and fought back an urge to tuck my head under my wing. I freely admit that I have never been the bravest of birds, and that apparition loomed larger than life itself.

'Hold out your hands,' the shadow repeated, and this time

Shoestring obeyed. The gloves came apart and the goat-man was gone.

If Shoestring had doubts, once the gloves were on his hands, all trace of hesitation disappeared. He leapt to his feet and, grabbing a bag, jumped over his friend and was out of the tent in an instant. The other boy, KidGlovz, followed immediately. I realised he'd been awake all along, lying quietly in the dark, listening to every word that was said. The dog went after both of them and I flew above all three, moving from tree to tree and staying out of sight.

At first Shoestring followed the road, then he set off on a path that I came to realise was as devious and twisted as his mind. He crisscrossed open fields and disappeared into thick forest before backtracking towards the town that we'd just left. When he came to some railway tracks he followed them. He moved with surprising speed and it was all I could do to keep up. KidGlovz and the dog were soon trailing behind.

I don't know the name of the town we ended up in. It was a big place, almost a city. I saw Shoestring move from house to house and I felt as if I wasn't so much watching one boy as tracking a strange partnership. Shoestring and the gloves worked together. Sometimes the gloves slipped off his hands and entered a building alone while he waited for them outside, holding the bag.

Other times he kept them on and used his old skills to scale a wall or slip through a high window. He was stealing,

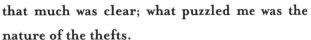

that much was clear; what puzzled me was the nature of the thefts.

I might be an old bird but I have sharp eyes and the things I saw him drop into the bag were not rings or cash or the valuable items you might expect, but rather objects of no great worth. I saw a book go in, followed by a candlestick and a toy horse. This intrigued me because, in the old days, Shoestring was the most selective of thieves and wouldn't dream of coming home without some precious find that would pass quickly across Mr Goldfiend's counter.

As the night wore on, I discovered that the objects Shoestring was collecting in his bag were simply souvenirs of his visit. What he was actually stealing was something entirely different.

# CHAPTER SEVENTEEN

# A Few Cards Short of a Deck

I BLINKED AND STARED, TRYING TO MAKE sense of what I saw. It was almost too much to comprehend. When Shoestring disappeared around the back of a rundown shack, leaving his bag lying open on the porch, I took the opportunity to peek inside and found a creased photo of a soldier, a cheap bangle and an ornament made of glass beads — trinkets that might have sentimental value but would be deemed worthless by Mr Goldfiend. I hopped aside and concealed myself in a shrub that grew against the splintered timbers of the wall as Shoestring climbed out the front window. He dropped a few measly coins in the bag, then he paused and sniffed the air.

'Metropolis,' he said softly. 'I was waiting for you to catch up. Why don't you step out into the open?'

I realised that he knew all along I was following him – after all, he had Lobe's sharp ears and could hear every beat of my wings.

'You can't hide from me, Metropolis,' he continued. 'I hear every breath you take, and with Hugo's sense of smell you reek like a chook house.'

There was no point in hiding so I hopped to the ground. Shoestring smiled. He spread his hands and the white gloves shone in the moonlight.

'Allow me to explain, Metropolis,' he said. 'Let me elucidate my actions and enlighten you as to my procurements.'

I don't know whose words he was using. I had never heard him speak like that before.

'Why have I taken these meagre coins?' he asked, and then answered his own question. 'The coins are merely a memento, a token to remind me that what I have stolen is a poor man's hope for the future. Do you understand?'

I shook my head.

'And this little wooden horse?' He picked the toy out of the bag and threw it in the air.

'It's a wish.' He laughed as he caught it. 'A child's dream of a pony. And the pen and the paintbrush? Calculations, dreams and speculation!' He tossed the objects back into the bag.

As he spoke, I heard KidGlovz and the dog catching up. *Stay back*, I thought. If I could have squawked I would have warned them, but I suppose it wouldn't have done any good;

Shoestring had no doubt heard them coming long before I had.

'Kid, my old friend!' he cried.

The footsteps stopped and I could hear the hound panting somewhere in the dark.

'I'm just explaining to Metropolis, to the *Macoa macaurus fabulosa*, the most curious and nosy of birds – always sticking her beak in where it's not wanted – how I can take whatever I desire – words, skills, and even people's hopes and dreams.'

I heard the wolfhound growl. I have to admit KidGlovz had more courage than me, because he stepped forward and stood before Shoestring, demanding to know what was going on.

'Nothing,' Shoestring replied. 'Naught, nil, zilch and zero, which, according to mathematical principles, is the smallest integer, the lowest ordinal number and the cardinality of the empty set.'

'It's those gloves. They're making you mad!' KidGlovz made a grab for Shoestring but the bigger boy slapped him aside.

'On the contrary, my dear Kid,' he replied. 'They're bringing me to my senses. I can hear what's going on all over the country. I can smell trouble from a mile off. And my night vision is one hundred per cent. Like them?' Shoe asked, staring wide-eyed at Kid. 'I took them from an owl.'

I was glad Shoestring was looking at KidGlovz and not me with those strange eyes. The pupils were large and dark and there was a hungry gleam in them. KidGlovz stood his ground. He stared back at his friend.

'Please stop, Shoe. Why are you doing this?'

'Because it's thrilling! The world is mine. I'm free to take whatever I like.'

'You're not free. The gloves have taken you over.'

I watched the dog edge forward with his ears flattened and his hackles raised. Shoestring ignored him and, dipping his hand in the bag, brought out a book.

'I took this for the inscription,' he said, casually tearing off the cover and hurling the rest of it over his shoulder. '*To Charlie. Forever yours*. What I've stolen is a promise.'

'Take off the gloves, Shoe. Take them off, right now!'

Shoestring laughed at the suggestion.

'When I tell May what you're up to she won't be proud of you anymore,' Kid said.

A worried look passed briefly over Shoestring's face, as if he had remembered something he would rather forget.

'You won't tell her anything.' He lowered his voice to a whisper. 'Because you won't be able to.'

A terrible cry filled the air when Shoestring reached for KidGlovz. I'm not sure if it came from Kid or the hound — perhaps it came from somewhere deep inside Shoestring himself.

I took flight at that moment. I wanted to get as far from the ground as possible. Not that the sky was safe — I knew those gloves could fly further and faster and higher than I could — but luckily they didn't follow.

When I dared to look down, Shoestring was gone. The front door of the shack was open and a man was bending over KidGlovz. I flapped into a bush near the shack and listened. I'm a solid bird as you know, round of girth and sound of mind, but you could have knocked me down with a feather once I realised what had happened.

'But where have you come from, boy?' the man asked. 'You must have a name.'

'Must have.' KidGlovz looked at the man, then turned his attention to the dog who was anxiously licking his hands. It's ghastly the way dogs lick but I think the hound was trying to help the boy.

'If I knew your name I might be able to find out where you live,' the man continued.

KidGlovz stroked the dog's ears. 'You're good,' he said, vaguely. 'Good dog. Your dog is good.'

'He's not my dog, he's yours.' The man scratched his head. 'Maybe your dog could take you home.'

'Home.' This word seemed to confuse KidGlovz, but the dog wasn't as foolish as he looked because he jumped up and wagged his tail as if he wanted to leave immediately. KidGlovz looked blank.

It began to rain so the fellow ushered them both onto his porch, which didn't offer much shelter as the roof was full of holes. They sat on a couple of old apple boxes.

'I had hopes of fixing up this place,' the man remarked, as the water dripped onto his lap. 'But it's a bit late in the day for that.'

'Late in the day,' Kid repeated, parrot-fashion.

The dog looked at the boy with sad eyes and occasionally gave him a nudge as if to wake him up. But KidGlovz wasn't asleep.

It was almost dawn. The man went inside and returned with bread and sausage, which he shared with his companions. I was feeling peckish and wouldn't have minded a bite myself, but I stayed out of sight. After a while the dog put his head under Kid's hand and when the boy grasped his collar he headed slowly down the street.

'Good day to you then,' the man said, shaking his head. 'Let's hope, when the sun comes up, you'll be right as rain.'

I'm normally not keen on dogs or children but I felt for those two. They headed off, the boy with his hand on the dog's collar and the hound with his nose to the ground. I could see the dog was trying to lead the boy back the way they'd come but he couldn't follow the scent. When they reached the end of the street he took a wrong turn. It was lucky I was there. I swooped in front of them and turned them around. Once they were back on the right track I flew a short distance ahead and waited for the dog to catch up. In this way, bit by bit, I guided them back to the troupe.

IT WAS LATE AFTERNOON BY THE TIME WE arrived.

When Lovegrove saw KidGlovz she raced to him and hugged him. 'There you are! We've been searching all day!'

May held out her arm and I landed on it like a falcon. 'Where's Shoestring? What happened?' she cried. Then she shook her head. 'If only you could talk, Metropolis.'

'Where did you go?' Lovegrove asked KidGlovz. 'You're so pale, Kid, and you're wet through. You look strange. Aren't you well?'

'Look strange,' the boy repeated. 'I feel a bit strange.' It was obvious to me that the kid was a few cards short of a deck, but Lovegrove thought he'd caught a chill.

# CHAPTER EIGHTEEN

# WHAT'S DONE IS DONE

LOVEGROVE WRAPPED KID IN A BLANKET and sat him by the fire.

'Poor little mite,' Grimwade said, holding a mug of soup out to the boy. 'He doesn't know his up from his down. Maybe he hit his head.'

Lovegrove examined Kid's head. 'I can't find any bumps.' She took the soup – KidGlovz didn't seem to know what to do with it. 'Are you all right?' she asked.

'Right as rain,' he replied.

*These people are kind*, Kid thought to himself.

When Lovegrove held the mug to his mouth, he drank some soup and thanked her.

'What's my name?' she asked. 'Do you know me?'

KidGlovz looked worried. He wanted to please the lady but he had no idea what her name was. He had no idea what his own name was.

'I'm Lovegrove,' she told him.

'Lovegrove. Thank you. I'll remember that.'

'You shouldn't have to remember. You've known me all your life!'

'All my life?' That was an interesting idea to KidGlovz, but one that was beyond his grasp. He couldn't imagine a before or an after. He was simply here with these people who seemed to know him. He watched a round-faced man prepare the meal and thanked Lovegrove again when she handed him a plate. He watched the others eat then he picked up his fork and copied them. They were all watching him. They seemed to be waiting for something.

'Let's try him with this,' Sylvie suggested when the meal was over. She handed KidGlovz his accordion.

When he held it upside down and played a few shaky notes, tears welled in Lovegrove's eyes. 'He's lost his music,' she whispered.

*He's lost his mind,* Sylvie thought, and she was trying to find a gentle way to tell Lovegrove this when Shoestring leapt out from behind the wagon.

'I'll show him how to play,' he cried. He grabbed the instrument and played a concerto KidGlovz had written for Sylvie. No notes were missing and although it was written for violin rather than accordion, it sounded magnificent.

'I didn't know you could play, Shoe.' May stepped towards him.

'I can now,' he laughed, and he launched into *Thin Air Sonata on a G-Minor String*.

'He's playing like Kid!' Sylvie cried. 'Stop it, Shoestring! Put it down.'

May grabbed the accordion. 'Get the gloves, Ace. Get them off him.'

Shoestring put up a struggle and it took several people to hold him.

When Ace tore the gloves from Shoestring's hands the boy yelled as if he was in pain. Ace threw the gloves into the fire and Shoestring stared after them, howling with despair.

'My gloves! My beautiful gloves!' He broke free and would have reached into the flames but Ace pulled him back.

'They're not burning!' Sylvie cried.

Everybody stared into the fire. The gloves had landed on a log and they lay there while the flames rose up around them. They looked like they were resting. Then, slowly, the fingers moved, reaching around the wood. They grabbed the burning log and hurled it at Ace. Everyone jumped back.

The troupe watched in disbelief as the gloves pulled the fire apart, scattering logs and burning sticks. Sparks showered everywhere. When the wood was gone the gloves scooped up handfuls of hot coals and threw them into the air. Then, empty-handed, they gave themselves a round of applause before flying away from the campsite.

'Come back!' Shoestring called after them. He tried to follow but Ace held him around the waist.

'Let them go. They're mad. *You're* mad.'

At the sound of Ace's voice, Shoestring stopped struggling and looked around him. Lovegrove and the Dittos were standing by the wagon, holding KidGlovz out of harm's way. They all looked shocked except for Kid, whose face was empty.

Ace loosened his grip and Shoestring sank to the ground. *What have I done?* he thought, as Lovegrove and the twins helped Kid into the back of the wagon.

'Put him to bed,' Lovegrove said. 'Maybe he'll feel better after a sleep. Sylvie, can you help the girls?'

Sylvie went to the wagon and climbed in with the others.

Nobody outside spoke for a long time. Grimwade rebuilt the fire. Shoestring got to his feet. He felt shaky and weak.

'Where are you going?' May said. 'Ace, stay with him.'

Shoestring walked slowly towards the wagon. He could see the children inside. Kid was tucked up in bed and the girls had their book open.

'That's you, Kid.' Daisy pointed to the page.

'I'm Kid?' KidGlovz studied his picture.

'And this is Shoestring.' Violet turned the page. 'He used to be your best friend.'

'I'm telling the story, Violet!' Daisy snatched the book away.

'Will you girls stop it?' Sylvie cried. 'We've got to work together here.'

Shoestring leaned on the tailgate and the girls looked up.

'Go away!' Sylvie yelled. 'You've caused enough trouble.'

Shoestring flinched as if he'd been hit. 'I'm sorry, Sylvie,' he said quietly. 'Kid, I'm sorry…'

KidGlovz looked up, puzzled. 'What for?' he asked.

'Come away from there.' Ace put his hand on Shoestring's shoulder. 'I don't know what's going on but we'll try and sort it out tomorrow.'

He led Shoestring to his tent and once his nephew was inside he turned to May.

'What are we to do?'

Shoe lay in the tent listening to May's thoughts, which were full of shame and regret. *What's happened to my boy?* she asked herself.

He heard Lovegrove's footsteps.

'I'm worried,' Lovegrove said. 'I fear for Sylvie and the others. There's no saying what Shoestring might do next.'

'I don't think he means it,' May said. 'I don't think he knows what he's doing.'

*He knows all right.* That was Metropolis. Even her thoughts were squawky.

'We need to make a decision.' Now Sylvie was there, beside them – little Sylvie, whom he loved like a sister. 'He'll have to go. We can't have him in the troupe. Look what he's done to Kid. It's not safe, Lovegrove.'

They were silent for a while, then Shoestring heard Lobe mutter his agreement.

May stifled a sob. 'All right, we'll take him home first thing tomorrow.'

*A fat lot of good that will do.* Metropolis again. How he hated that macaw! *Get rid of the boy. Send him away!*

Shoestring's head ached. He hardly knew if he was awake or asleep. He closed his eyes and felt soft fingers massaging his temples.

'That's so unfair,' came the whispery voice of the gloves, 'to banish a boy from his own troupe. It's unforgivable.'

Shoestring shook the hands off and sat up in the tent. His chest hurt and tears pricked his eyes. He thought of KidGlovz and a sob rose in his throat. He swallowed it back down and felt around for a candle. When he lit it he saw a bag lying at his feet. He opened it and tipped the contents onto the blanket, then one by one he picked things up.

He couldn't believe what he had done. He remembered the good old days when he was an innocent thief and the most valuable thing he'd ever taken was a gold watch. Now he could probably steal time itself if the gloves were on his hands. He gave a sigh and tears rolled down his face. Then he heard a familiar voice.

'No tears, my friend. We have work to do.'

Shoestring raised his head. The shadow loomed large on the wall of the tent.

'Go away. I'm finished with you!' he cried.

'Finished? My dear, we've only just begun.'

'I hate you. Get away from me!'

'But I'm your friend, your servant. I'm a pair of willing hands.'

'You're not even a person. You're just a shape on the wall. You made me do terrible things.'

Shoestring blew out the candle so he didn't have to see that awful silhouette. That didn't stop the shadow talking.

'Rubbish, my boy. You're overwrought. Pop the gloves on this instant!'

'You can't tell me what to do,' Shoestring said, and he meant it.

There was some rustling in the dark, then the candle was relit.

'Quite right,' the shadow said. 'You should be telling *me* what to do. I'm your servant and your wish is my command.'

'Give Kid back his memory!' Shoestring demanded.

'Impossible! What's done is done!'

Shoestring stood up. He was as tall as the shadow.

'Give it back!' he cried. 'Give everything back!'

Whack! Shoestring felt the gloves slap him to the ground and for a while he knew nothing. He didn't see the gloves pick up the things that were scattered on the blanket and he didn't see them put everything back in the bag.

'I'll take these stolen goods and put them away for safekeeping,' the shadowy voice said. 'I'll lock them in the strongroom until you wake up to yourself.'

'I am awake.' Shoestring struggled to his feet but the gloves knocked him down as soon as he stood up.

'You're trying me, boy.' The voice took on a dangerous note. 'What's this then?'

The gloves grabbed Shoestring's mirror and pulled him up by it until he was standing on tiptoes.

'It's just a trinket. May gave it to me…'

Shoe tried to sound as if he didn't care about the mirror, as if he hadn't worn it over his heart, as if he didn't think of May every time he held it.

'It's nothing, just a little—'

'Oh, your beloved May. I'll have that!' The gloves reefed the mirror from Shoestring's neck and he fell back to the ground.

'Farewell, my friend!' they cried as they flew away with the bag.

Part Four

# CHAPTER NINETEEN

# On the Road

TALK ABOUT SULLEN! IF SHOESTRING HAD regretted his actions the night before, all trace of that regret was gone by morning. He didn't care about May anymore. He didn't care about anyone. He studied the map on the back of his invitation and paced up and down, eager to be on the road.

May was packing her suitcases.

'I've never seen him like this,' she said. 'He's holding his cards much too close to his chest. Watch him, Ace. Don't let him out of your sight until we get back to Cadenza.'

I don't know what May expected to happen when we reached the Luck Palace. It wasn't as if Shoestring would come good just because we were inside the door. I'd seen him in action. I knew what the gloves could do. It was enough to have lost my voice; if the gloves returned I could end up losing my wits like KidGlovz had — we all could end up like that.

'COME ON,' SHOESTRING YELLED. 'WE SHOULD
have left by now.'

'You can forget about going to the festival,' May said. 'We're
taking you home.'

If Shoestring woke in a worse state that morning, KidGlovz
seemed slightly improved. He had some colour in his cheeks
and when Lovegrove looked in the wagon he knew her name.

'Hello, Lovegrove,' he said.

'You remember me!'

'Yes. Here you're on page thirteen with Hugo.' Kid pointed
to the Dittos' book. 'And here's Grimwade and Shoestring and
Ace and Sylvie. I'm learning them all.' He turned to the girls.
'It's a true story, isn't it?'

'Yes, Kid,' Sylvie replied. 'It's the story of your life.'

Lovegrove tried to hide her disappointment. She gave
KidGlovz his breakfast and told him to rest.

May and Ace packed up and when the wagon was loaded,
Grimwade took the reins and the troupe headed towards the
station. They hadn't gone far when they met a wagon with
a painted sign across the front that said THE GREAT ALEXIS –
AIRWALKER EXTRAORDINAIRE.

Alexis was not a young man, but he was fine as a wire and
his muscles rippled like steel cables. He leapt to the ground as
soon as he saw Shoestring's banner.

'I've heard of you,' he cried, shaking Shoestring's hand.
'Every skywalker, aerial artist and funambulist from the

western mountains to the eastern seaboard has your name on their lips. I'm thrilled to meet you.

'But why are you heading in the wrong direction? The festival is this way.' He pointed ahead. 'Straight up the north road then turn east at Five-Ways Junction. It's about two weeks' journey from here.'

Shoestring hung his head. 'I'm not allowed to go.'

'What?' The Great Alexis looked around accusingly. 'You're not competing in the Festival of Marvels, when you may well be the greatest marvel of all? That's ridiculous!'

'That's how it is,' Shoestring said, kicking the dust.

'The boy's not right,' Grimwade explained. 'There's something amiss with him.'

'Tragic.' Alexis jumped back on his wagon. 'But now, at least the other competitors may have a chance.'

Shoestring grew more agitated after the encounter. He took out his rope and walked beside the wagon, flicking it over Haul's head in an annoying way that made the horse snort and swish his tail. When May asked him to stop, he began cracking the rope like a stockwhip, which upset Haul even more.

'I want to go to the festival,' he muttered. 'It's not fair.'

May took the rope from him and locked it in the box seat of the wagon. Then she sat on the lid and Shoestring sat next to her. Metropolis didn't want to be near him. She left May and flew into the back, landing on Daisy's shoulder.

'Sit on *my* shoulder, Metropolis, not hers,' her sister said.

'She chose me, Violet.'

Sylvie gently lifted Metropolis onto her own shoulder. 'Finish the story,' she said. They were near the end of the book.

Violet flicked through the pages and stopped at a picture of KidGlovz performing in a grand concert hall.

'That's you, Kid,' she said.

Kid sighed. 'It's hard to believe I could play like that.'

'Maybe you will again,' Sylvie said softly, although she didn't think it was likely.

Lobe and Ace were playing cards on the other side of the wagon. 'He'd have to start from scratch,' Ace said.

'Sad, isn't it?' Lobe said to Ace. 'I've lost my hearing but that poor kid has lost the lot.'

'I wish we could help him,' Daisy said.

'I do too,' said Violet.

The twins looked at each other in surprise.

'At least we agree on something!' they said.

KidGlovz took little notice of the people around him. He flipped back through the pages of the book. 'I like Hugo,' he said. 'And I like Mot, even if he's grumpy.'

'Who's he talking about?' Ace asked.

'Just some character in the story,' Lobe replied. 'Get on with the game.'

'He's a hermit,' Daisy said. 'He lives on Goat Mountain. He can dream the answer to any question in the world.'

The girls stared at each other. There was a long silence before Violet spoke, and what she said startled both of them.

'Are you thinking what I'm thinking?'

Daisy looked deep into her sister's eyes. 'Yes, I am,' she said. 'Stop! Stop the wagon!'

'What's up?' Grimwade called.

'We need to go to Goat Mountain!'

The twins almost knocked Metropolis aside in their hurry to get out. They leapt over the tailboard and ran around the front. Sylvie and Lovegrove followed with the book.

*That's right, just ignore Metropolis,* the macaw thought as she flapped after them.

'Whoa up, Haul. Halt!' Grimwade yelled.

'Page 176.' The Dittos pointed to the picture.

Lovegrove didn't want to get her hopes up but she stared hard at the drawing of Mot. 'Do you really think he could help Kid?' she asked.

'He did last time,' the girls chimed.

May stroked her chin. 'If this fellow can dream the answers, maybe he can tell us how to help Shoe as well.'

'I don't need any help,' Shoestring said.

GOAT MOUNTAIN WAS IN A REMOTE western part of the country, but to get there the troupe first had to go north. Grimwade turned the wagon around. This pleased Shoestring because that was the way The Great Alexis had gone.

As they travelled along, the road became crowded with people heading towards the festival. There were wagons, donkey carts, food carts and people on foot.

When the troupe was overtaken by a group of aerialists called the Altitudinous Tumblers, Shoestring slipped to the ground. He ran ahead and struck up a conversation. He wanted to hitch a ride but May refused to give him his rope.

'Maybe you should let him have it,' Ace suggested.

Metropolis had the same idea. She nodded vehemently. *We'd all be safer if Shoestring wasn't with us*, she thought.

May shook her head. 'We've got to look after him,' she muttered.

THERE'S A LOT TO BE SAID FOR THE WIDER view. Any high-flying bird with a half-decent wingspan will tell you that. I flew above and checked out the traffic.

It soon became obvious that the Jubilee Festival of Marvels was going to be an enormous event. Tightrope performers weren't the only people heading towards Five-Ways Junction; there were fire eaters, tumblers, strongmen, musicians, sword swallowers and all manner of acrobats, as well as wagons selling wares — traders who'd come for the crowds, which promised to be huge.

There was an air of excitement about the travellers. I flew among them, gleaning bits of information. At Five-Ways Junction people would take the Tuffa Road to North Caldera; the festival was somewhere near there. There were rumours that it had been organised to celebrate the birthday of the patron, but nobody seemed to know who that was. There was also much talk about the main event, which promised to be challenging. The drop, over which the tightrope walkers were to perform, was like no other, and many said they would decide whether or not they would compete once they arrived. It would depend on the weather conditions, the wind speed and the updraught. Some people said the rope would be strung over a huge waterfall that tumbled over a breathtaking cliff face, others claimed it would be strung over a bottomless pit.

I couldn't tell May what I'd heard but no doubt she found out by herself. We set up camp that evening on open ground by the roadside. Several wagons were already parked there and more stopped as it grew dark. Most had painted signs. I read the names: MISS LILLY WHITE'S ODDITORIUM — UNBELIEVABLE ANATOMICAL WONDERS. HIGH-FLYING PHILLIPO. THE LEGENDARY FLAMBÉ. DR ARMADILLO'S MIRACLE PILLS — CURE WHAT AILS YOU!

Shoestring was excited by the activity. He ran among the wagons looking for Alexis, but he didn't find him. When May tried to make him sit down and eat, he pushed the food away.

'Aren't you hungry?' Grimwade asked.

'Yes, but not for food,' Shoe muttered.

I don't think Grimwade heard him, but I did. That night I chose to roost high up in a tree. I didn't like the look on the boy's face and May can't have liked it either.

'You'll sleep in my tent tonight,' she told Shoestring. 'With Ace on one side and me on the other.'

<hr />

SHOE SLEPT DEEPLY AND THE GLOVES FLEW through his dreams. He saw them flying over mountains and sweeping low over forests. They passed towns, farms and villages until they reached the campsite where he lay waiting for them.

He lifted his head as they flew through the tent flap; with a rush of excitement, he sat up and held out his hands. He felt the familiar thrill as the gloves slipped on. Then somebody stirred beside him and he woke with a start — and found his

hands were bare. His joy turned to bitter disappointment. With a deep sigh he turned over and went back to sleep.

The next morning there were even more people on the road. May and Ace were worn out; they hadn't slept. May glanced nervously at Shoestring but he seemed calm, so she let herself nod off on Ace's shoulder. She stirred when the troupe reached Five-Ways Junction. Sylvie read the names on the sign: WARPING MINOR, GOAT MOUNTAIN, TUFFA, HOLLOWAY FLATS, ARC RIVER.

Grimwade suggested they spend the night at Five-Ways because the campsite was good and there was plenty of grass nearby for Haul.

Shoestring stood watching all the wagons turning off towards Tuffa.

*I could go without my rope*, he thought, *but then I'd just be like any other tightrope walker.*

May had started unpacking. 'I need my rope,' he told her.

'I'm sorry, Shoe. I'm not giving it to you. We'll go and see this Mr Mot and then maybe you can have it back.'

Shoestring rattled the padlock.

'Leave it, boy. Go and help May set up the tent,' Ace said.

'Help her yourself.' Shoestring walked away. He would find a pin and pick the lock as soon as he got the chance.

LOBE SLEPT ON THE WAGON SEAT THAT night, guarding the padlock. I found the highest tree I could. I told myself that if there was trouble I should look after number one, but I was worried about May, so after a while I flew down to her tent and poked my head under the flap. Shoestring was asleep but May was wide awake and so was Ace. They motioned for me to get out of the way and I saw they were not empty-handed. If I had a voice I would have advised May to arm herself with something more substantial than Daisy Ditto's butterfly net. What did she think she was doing? The boy was dangerous. He had a criminal streak. He wasn't some moth they could catch in a net.

I cringed and pressed myself against the wall of the tent when the gloves flew inside. They fluttered about, finding matches and candle, but before they could strike a light, May and Ace were upon them. May swiped at a glove and with one twist of the wrist she had it trapped in her butterfly net.

I realised I'd underestimated her. She knew what she was about; she'd caught the glove before Shoestring even stirrred.

'Stop it!' he cried. A moment later Ace caught its partner. May handed Ace her net and watched while he stuffed both gloves into Sylvie's violin case. He closed the lid and locked it, then he took off his belt and tied it around the case before strapping it to his back.

THE NEXT MORNING GRIMWADE SUGGESTED
we get rid of the gloves and I wholeheartedly agreed. 'We can
weight the case with a rock and dump it in the first river we
come across,' he said.

Shoestring went pale. He was standing behind Ace with his
eyes fixed on the case.

'I've had that violin case all my life, Mr Grimwade,' Sylvie
said. 'I don't want to lose it. Besides, if the gloves won't burn
they probably won't drown either.'

Shoestring looked relieved.

'Sylvie's right,' Madame Lovegrove said. 'Let's take the
gloves to the hermit man and ask him what to do with them.'

May checked that the violin case was strapped securely
before we set off. Shoestring's eyes never left Ace's back.
There was no risk of him leaving the troupe now. The gloves
held him. Wherever Ace was, Shoestring was close behind,
watching.

# CHAPTER TWENTY

# THE HERMIT

MOT, THE HERMIT, WAS SICK TO DEATH OF answering questions. Each day was the same, an endless row of people seeking his advice. And the nights were no better because as soon as he put down his head he was visited by dreams, one after another, all the way until morning. He always woke exhausted. It wasn't fair. He hadn't chosen this profession; the job was a nightmare and he wanted out.

'Go away, you fools,' he yelled as he stomped to the door. He looked out and saw the queue was longer than ever. It stretched halfway down the mountain and now there was a wagon at the end of it. It was parked right next to his **KEEP OUT** sign. He sighed and went back inside his hut, slamming the door behind him.

'Next!' he yelled.

A farmer came in wanting to know if he should plant his crop early that year.

'Will it rain in September?' he asked.

'I'll sleep on it,' Mot replied. 'Next!'

A worried fellow entered the hut and told the hermit he'd had two marriage proposals and didn't know which one to accept. Mot groaned.

'Make up your own mind,' he said. 'Next!'

The door opened and closed. He didn't even bother looking up.

'Question?' he asked.

'My son's bone lazy and I'm sick of him.'

'Not a question,' Mot said. 'Next!'

'It's going to be a long wait,' Sylvie said to the lady in front of her.

'I've been waiting for months,' the woman replied. 'But it will be worth it. He's very wise.'

Shoestring's eyes flicked from the violin case to the woman's face.

*I'm not waiting*, he thought.

'If Mot doesn't know the answer to your question he'll go to sleep and dream it. Then he'll paint it on the wall of his hut,' the woman told Sylvie. 'But he's a bit mad.'

'Clear out – all of you!' they heard Mot yell.

'He doesn't mean that,' the woman said. 'It's his job, answering questions.'

'This is going to take ages,' Grimwade said. 'Let's play Patience.'

'Or Royal Flush,' May suggested. 'How many sets of cards did you bring, Ace?'

**I**T DIDN'T TAKE MAY LONG TO GET SOME CARD games going. Grimwade made a fire and people came towards the light to try their hand. May taught them the rules and the atmosphere on Goat Mountain changed from one of listless waiting to something so reminiscent of the Luck Palace that I felt a little twinge under my left breast feathers, nothing serious – I think it was a touch of homesickness.

People talked and laughed and for every player in a game, six or seven more were waiting to take their turn. May wondered if the Dittos might provide some entertainment and asked Sylvie to play, but the child's violin was still off-key and the twins, despite their earlier accord on the subject of KidGlovz, couldn't agree on what dance they would do, so the idea was abandoned.

It didn't matter. Before long, one of the players – a rough-looking fellow in a goatskin coat – hit the jackpot and burst into song:

'Fate dealt me a hand and my luck went wild.

I turned up a card and the joker smiled...'

He was probably a shepherd. He had a yodelling sort of voice that rang across the mountain and the high notes went right through you. It wasn't my kind of song but the assorted company enjoyed it well enough and joined in with a rousing chorus, stamping their feet in time with the music. Soon the place was as busy as a good night at the Luck Palace.

As you know, I'm a bird with an enquiring mind. I flew among the stalls and soon sized up the situation on Goat Mountain. All manner of people had come there to ask Mot their questions — farmers, shopkeepers, teachers, shepherds, blacksmiths, bakers, carpenters and potters. Some had been waiting so long they'd set up shop.

Among their ranks was a forlorn-looking fellow with a load of old leather-bound books. The name on the cart was Illuminati, but he was a lame duck, I could tell. He stood on the sidelines watching the card games and he seemed half asleep, but every now and then he would rouse himself and yell to no one in particular, '*The Sum of Human Knowledge* going cheap!' When Sylvie made her way towards him he looked surprised, as if he never expected anyone to answer his call.

'Have you been waiting long?' she asked.

'Forever,' he replied.

'What's your question for the hermit?'

I landed on his cart and cocked my head.

Mr Illuminati gestured towards his books and told Sylvie that he'd been hauling them around for years and had never sold a single volume. He wanted to ask the hermit for help.

'Can I have a look?' she asked.

'Be my guest.'

Sylvie put on her spectacles and read the first few volumes in the time it takes Ace to shuffle a pack of cards.

'You're a fast reader,' Mr Illuminati remarked.

'Yes,' she replied, without looking up. 'I'm a prodigy.'

He looked along his books and picked a volume. Then he opened it up and ran his finger down the page. 'Prodigy. "A genius child possessed of unusual or marvellous talents,"' he read. '"The prodigy, or wunderkind, may have remarkable skills in a particular area…"'

'With me it's mainly music,' Sylvie interrupted, 'but I can do other things. I can remember everything I read.'

'Really? Let me test you.' Mr Illuminati opened one of the books Sylvie had finished. He closed his eyes and pointed randomly. 'Air?' he asked.

'The invisible elastic substance that surrounds the earth, the properties of which consist of nitrogen (78.09%), oxygen (20.95%), carbon dioxide (0.039%) with traces of hydrogen, helium and other noble gases.'

'That's amazing.' Mr Illuminati raised his hat and watched while Sylvie read the rest of the encyclopedia. He was so impressed that when he next called out '*The Sum of Human Knowledge* going cheap!' there was some new enthusiasm in his voice that attracted attention he'd never got before. A crowd gathered around the cart.

A little gasp came from the audience and a lady held up her hand.

'Yes?' Sylvie asked.

'Tell us about infinity.'

'From the Latin *infinitas*, meaning unlimited, boundless, without end. In mathematics it means a number greater than any assignable quantity. See *infinitesimal calculus*, Volume X.'

The crowd applauded.

'What a brilliant child,' the lady said to Mr Illuminati. 'How does she know all this?'

The bookseller spread his hands. 'She's read *The Sum of*

*Human Knowledge*,' he cried. 'Madam, would you like to buy a set?'

The woman said she would, and so did several other people in the crowd. Soon a queue formed at the wagon. Everyone was lining up to buy encyclopedias.

Mr Illuminati couldn't believe his luck. 'What's your name, little girl?' he asked.

'Sylvie Quickfingers.'

I didn't stay to see what happened after that. I flew over the heads of the people then flapped my way along the side of the queue until I reached Mot's hut. He was looking out the door and I landed at his feet.

'You again,' he sighed, although he'd never seen me before.

A man at the front of the line nudged me aside with his boot and spoke to Mot.

'They've got a kid who's lost his mind and the boy who's stolen it. And a pair of gloves locked in a violin case. There's a little girl...'

'Gloves?' Mot cried. 'Send them up!'

ALL OF US CROWDED INTO MOT'S SMALL HUT. I sat on Lobe's head because he was the tallest. The hermit looked each of us over and his eyes rested on Shoestring.

'I knew you would come back,' he muttered. 'You're going to take my place.'

Shoestring looked confused. 'What did you say?'

'You heard me.'

Lovegrove came forward holding KidGlovz in front of her. 'Mr Mot, what are you talking about? We've come to ask you a question.'

'That's all I ever get!' The hermit threw his hands in the air. 'Questions! Well, the answer's in the thread.'

They say I'm a bad-tempered bird but, believe me, I'm a sweet little chickadee compared with that Mot. A simple statement like that and he flew off the handle.

Lovegrove was taken back.

'What?' she said. 'We haven't asked anything yet.'

'Don't you people listen?' Mot cried. 'The answer is in the thread!'

It was obvious that the fellow was out of his tree. He was making as much sense as a headless turkey.

'The gloves are made of two things – cloth and thread,' the lunatic shouted. 'I'm telling you what I told her. *The answer is in the thread!*'

I could see May was inclined to pick him up and throw him out of his own hut – but she wasn't in the Luck Palace now, so she controlled herself and spoke to him in a civil fashion.

'Told who? What are you saying? We haven't even asked you about the gloves …'

'Hermits-on-high save us!' Mot rolled his eyes. 'All of you idiots, sit down,' he said. 'I'll try and spell it out.'

There was nowhere to sit. Mot's chair was the only one in the hut.

'For years I was plagued with questions about a pair of white gloves,' he said. 'They were out every full moon causing havoc. People wanted to know how to protect themselves.' Mot closed his eyes and sighed. 'Then one day, somebody caught them and brought them to me. She was called Marm,' Mot said.

Marm! When I heard that name I raised my crest and dug my claws deep into Lobe's scalp. May gasped. We looked at each other and we looked at the hermit.

'She wanted to know how to master them,' he cried. 'I dreamed the answer. I told her what I'm telling you.' He jumped to his feet and began singing a sort of chant.

*"Tween Twixt and Twirl and kith and kin*
*Split the light and spin and spin*
*The river winds by Warp on Twine*
*Ply the thread with hair so fine ...'*

'What's that supposed to mean?' Lovegrove asked. 'You haven't answered our question.'

'You haven't asked it,' the hermit yelled.

'This boy's lost his memory. How do we get it back?'

Mot groaned. 'Can't you people listen!'

He repeated the rhyme and while he was doing that I took the liberty of inspecting the murals that decorated the walls of his hut. There were scenes from thousands of lives. Some of the pictures were obscured by smoke from the old man's cooking fire and in a dark corner of the hut behind the stove I thought I saw a cherry, a painted one of course, but the colour drew my eye. When I flapped towards it I found it wasn't a cherry but a gleaming red stone. The hand that held it had long, shiny fingernails. My blood ran cold. It was Marm.

I hovered near the wall, trying to take in the picture. Mot was still chanting but I could barely hear him above the beating of my heart.

'... *The river winds by Warp on Twine. Ply the thread...* Would someone control that wretched bird?' he yelled.

May came over and provided me with her shoulder and we both stared at Marm's image. She was standing behind a woman who was spinning. The woman had long plaited hair and wore a beautiful woven shawl. Marm was in shadow but the stone in her hand shone brightly. It was the Eye of the Dragon and the light was shining through it in coloured rays. The woman was spinning the shafts of light and winding the thread onto her spindle.

'Lordy!' May gasped. 'Did you dream this? What's it about?'

Sylvie and the others came to look.

'The diamond's acting as a prism,' young Sylvie said. 'It's splitting the light into all the colours of the spectrum.'

May gulped and stared. 'Oh, Metropolis,' she breathed, and when she turned to me, something in her face reminded me of that frightened fourteen-year-old. 'I thought our past was behind us,' she said.

So had I. But now it had surfaced and pictures ran before my eyes – not the ones on the wall of Mot's hut, but the ones inside my mind. I think May saw them too.

They say when you're about to die your whole life flashes before you. I was back in the cage in the House of Diamonds

and I was watching Marm's son. I remember that day as if it was yesterday. Jack Diamond was prising a stone from the entrance hall. He looked up and saw me and then calmly, ever so calmly, slid open the drawer of the table on which my cage was placed and took out the key. I saw him unlock the little door and as he reached towards me I didn't even squawk. What could I do? I was a sitting duck. But just before his fingers reached my throat a bird whistled somewhere high above in the lofty spaces of the ceiling. Jack looked up. He only turned his head for a second, but that was all the time it took for him to be struck by a shooting star. A diamond the size of a paperweight hit him straight between the eyes and killed him stone dead.

I looked up and saw May teetering at the top of the ladder. Then I hopped out of the cage and flapped across the floor. I'd been so long in captivity I could barely fly. I watched May make her descent and when she reached the bottom rung I sighed with relief. She stepped to the ground, her eyes wide with fright. She was shaking so much she could hardly undo the bunch of keys that hung from Jack Diamond's belt.

Before we left the House of Diamonds, May took the cards from my cage and scooped up a handful of precious stones, putting them in her pocket.

'For our future, Metropolis,' she whispered, and then she picked me up and ran.

We raced through the mining town and down the mountain.

May was tiny and thin but she ran swiftly through the night. At one stage she stumbled and when she did I took to the air.

'Follow me!' I cried.

All night May ran, and I managed to fly ahead of her. She ran until she could go no further, and when she stopped I circled back and landed on her shoulder.

'I didn't mean to kill him, Metropolis,' she panted.

'It's behind us, May. Forget it. We'll never speak of it again.' I pointed my beak at the night sky. 'The future is ahead,' I said. 'Look.'

There was a bright star shining over the horizon, just like the one on the card.

◇◇◇◇◇◇◇◇◇◇◇◇◇◇◇◇◇◇◇◇◇◇◇◇◇◇◇◇◇◇◇◇◇◇◇◇◇◇◇◇◇◇◇◇◇◇◇◇◇◇◇◇◇◇◇

'WHAT CAN I DO TO MAKE YOU PEOPLE understand?' Mot cried. 'How many times do I have to chant that wretched rhyme? *The river winds by Warp on Twine. Ply the—*'

'This is not helping KidGlovz,' Lovegrove interrupted.

'Or Shoestring,' Ace added.

'What's the name of this lady?' Sylvie asked, pointing to the picture.

'Braid.' The hermit flopped back in his chair. 'Next!' he yelled.

'We're not leaving,' Ace told him. 'Not until we get some answers.'

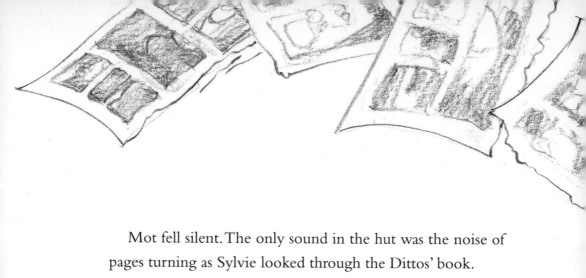

Mot fell silent. The only sound in the hut was the noise of pages turning as Sylvie looked through the Dittos' book.

'Mr Mot, are these the gloves you're talking about?' she asked.

'Who wrote that?' Mot was on his feet in a second. He grabbed the book and flipped through it in a rage.

'Since this story was printed the whole world knows about me. That's why the queues are so long. Thousands of people have come looking for answers. I get no peace.'

He tore the book in half, ripping out pages and throwing them into the air.

'I've had enough of you people,' the hermit yelled. 'GET OUT!'

'He's flipped,' Ace said. 'He's lost the plot. Come on, let's go.'

May was still staring at the wall in shock. She put one hand on her shoulder, covering Metropolis's foot.

If Ace hadn't taken her arm she might not have moved. He led her from the hut.

'Do you know that lady?' he asked.

She didn't reply.

Sylvie walked beside Ace. 'Maybe Mot hasn't lost the plot,' she said quietly. 'A lady called Braid who spins…'

She chanted the rhyme as they headed back down the hill.

*'Tween Twixt and Twirl and kith and kin*
*Split the light and spin and spin*
*The river winds by Warp on Twine*
*Ply the thread with hair so fine…'*

'I think it's a riddle,' she said when they reached the wagon.

The troupe began packing up. Ace went around the groups of card players and collected the packs. 'Time to go,' he told them. 'Game's over.'

Lobe harnessed Haul, and Grimwade put away his cooking pots. May didn't help. She sat on the seat of the wagon with Metropolis on her lap.

'I should have guessed,' she said. 'Marm wants to punish me, to punish us.'

She stroked Metropolis to steady her trembling hands and then she took out her cards and shuffled them. She drew one from the pack. It was The Goat.

'Shoestring will reach great heights,' she said, trying to

reassure herself. 'There's no danger. He'll be sure-footed as a mountain goat.'

Metropolis raised her crest. The card was upside down. Couldn't May see that? When the card is upside down the meaning is reversed!

**M**AY NEVER DID GET THE hang of reading the cards. She learned the names — The Goat, The Twins, The Thief, The Rising Star, The Arrow — but she was only reciting them parrot-fashion and had no real sense of their meaning. And she could no more put two cards together than fly over the moon. I couldn't understand it. She'd watched me often enough and I'd tried to teach her many times. In fact, I'd started forty years ago. During those first few months after our escape from the House of Diamonds, May and I stopped in the marketplace of every town we passed through. We worked as a team. She would lay out the spread and I would interpret. We never stayed longer than three days.

As our business grew May experimented with other cards — not the Cards of Life, just ordinary playing cards — and she found that was where her talent lay. She quickly learned to play Crazy Eights, Black Jack, Grand Sham and Dead Man's Hand before moving on to Royal Flush and Blind Man's

Bluff, two games of her own invention that became popular in gaming halls and card parlours throughout the land. She rarely lost a game. With my feather tucked in her cap she said she couldn't lose. She claimed it acted as a lightning rod, bringing down the luck.

But now her luck had run out. I could see it in her face. I took the card and put it back in the pack, then I hopped on her shoulder and gave her a little peck on the cheek to comfort her. She hardly noticed.

Ace came and stood beside us, looking at May with concern. Shoestring was right behind him.

'What is it, May?' he asked. 'Who was that woman in the picture?'

She gave a deep sigh. 'It's history, Ace. Someone we used to know.'

◇◇◇◇◇◇◇◇◇◇◇◇◇◇◇◇◇◇◇◇◇◇◇◇◇◇◇◇◇◇◇◇◇◇◇◇◇◇◇◇◇◇◇◇◇◇◇◇◇◇◇◇◇◇◇◇◇

MAY HAD LEFT MR GOLDFIEND IN CHARGE of the Luck Palace. Trying to manage the shop downstairs and keep the upstairs business going as well meant he barely had a spare moment, so despite his numerous contacts, it was some time before he tracked down the information May had requested. He came home one evening and shared what he had learned with Ruby, who was minding the counter.

'It seems Mistress Adamantine was once a big name in the diamond world but then she disappeared. Apparently her son was killed by a servant girl and after that the woman closed the mine.'

Ruby frowned. She was cleaning the glass window of the display cabinet in which Mr Goldfiend stored the watches.

'She got rid of all her staff except for her bodyguards,' Goldfiend continued. 'And then she lived as a recluse among her diamonds, swearing to avenge her son's death. That was forty years ago. No one has heard of her since.'

'May was that servant.' Ruby put both hands on the counter. 'Marm was terrible even then, I can't imagine what she'd be like now.'

Mr Goldfiend raised his eyebrows. 'If May had left a forwarding address I'd write advising her to steer well clear of the woman.'

'No need,' said Ruby. 'If May never saw Mistress Adamantine again, it would be too soon.'

'ALL ABOARD!' GRIMWADE YELLED WHEN the wagon was packed. He clicked his tongue and Haul moved off. We headed back along the road on which we'd come, waved off by a disappointed crowd. People were sorry to see us go and they looked dejected as they returned to their place in the queue.

May was quiet. She stared at the road and her face was full of dread. If I'd had a voice I would have filled the silence.

I would have reminded her that all was not lost, that we'd seen grim times before — in fact our friendship was forged in the worst of situations — and look how far we'd come! Look at the Luck Palace!

You may be wondering how a poor street girl with a flair for card-playing and a smart-talking macaw could end up with such a grand establishment. Well, it was a matter of our little nest egg. I could see those precious stones would burn a hole in May's pocket, so I advised her to invest immediately. As soon as we arrived in Cadenza city I flew to the top end of town and picked up some vital information regarding stocks, bonds, securities and futures, much as an ordinary bird might raid an orchard, then, with the help of the well-connected Mr Goldfiend, whose sixth sense for profit bordered on the prophetic, our future was assured. Some time after that Ruby found us and May offered her a job.

'You never know what's around the next corner, May,' I wanted to say, but with no voice to cheer her I remained silent. Grimwade slapped the reins and Haul broke into a trot. We hadn't gone far when I heard somebody yelling. I flapped up onto the roof of the wagon and saw it was that fellow who'd sold the encyclopedias. He was running along behind us.

'Wait!' he called. 'Sylvie, wait!'

'Whoa up!' Grimwade said and Haul came to a halt. The man held up an atlas.

'Sylvie, I want to give you a present. There are no encyclopedias left but would you like this?'

Sylvie leaned over the tailboard and took the book. 'Thank you, Mr Illuminati!'

'Good luck!' The fellow stood and waved and I watched him until we went around a bend. From there the road headed steeply downhill. I had the uneasy feeling that we'd need more than luck to see us through the next leg of that fateful journey.

LOOM

TWINE VALLEY

WARPING MINOR

WARPING

TWINE RIVE

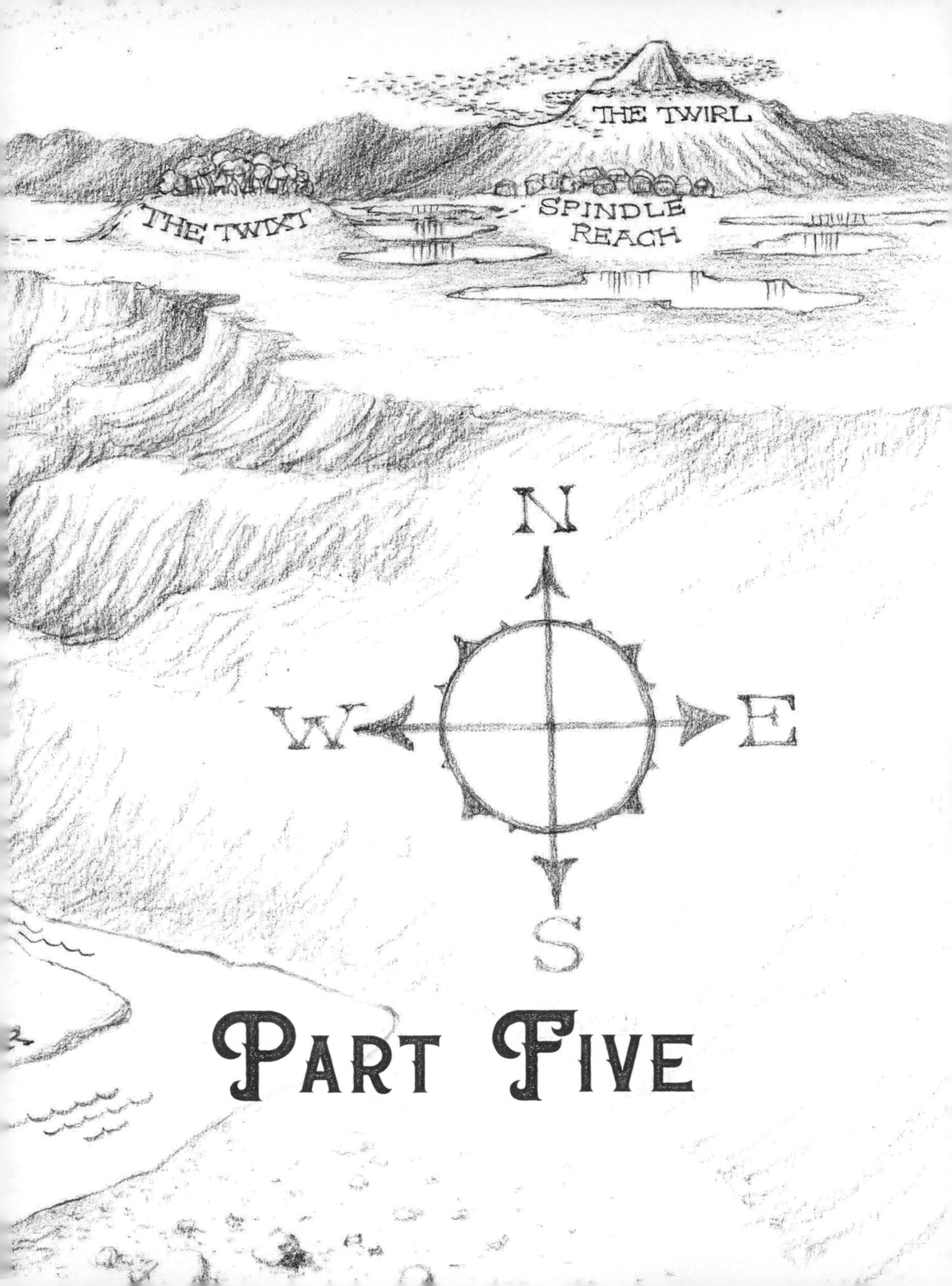

THE TWIRL

THE TWIXT

SPINDLE
REACH

N

W E

S

# Part Five

CHAPTER TWENTY-ONE

# TWINE VALLEY

SYLVIE SAT ON THE FRONT SEAT WITH THE
atlas open. 'There's a place called Warping Minor on the Twine
River. I think we should go that way.'

'Why, Sylvie?' Lovegrove asked.

'Because it's in the riddle and Braid could be there. If we
find her she might be able to help.'

The troupe travelled all day, following Sylvie's directions,
and when they reached a signpost that pointed east to Twine
River Valley and Loom, and west to Five-Ways Junction, they
turned east.

'That's the wrong way,' Shoestring said. 'Let's go towards
Five-Ways.' His eyes narrowed. 'I'm going to miss the festival
at this rate,' he muttered, and the further they went the more
desperate he felt.

When Ace travelled in the back of the wagon, Shoestring
did too. If the road grew steep and Ace got out and walked
to make the going easier for Haul, Shoestring walked as well.
When Ace sat on the front seat, Shoestring stood on the

bargeboard behind him. He stared so hard at the violin case Ace could almost feel the gaze boring through his back.

'Give it a rest, boy,' he said. But Shoestring couldn't rest.

*I want out of here,* Shoe thought. *But I'm not leaving without my gloves and my rope.*

Ace felt safest inside the wagon where he could lean against the wall. He was getting jumpy and he asked Lobe to watch his back. Everyone was relieved when they saw the Twine River in the distance. Sylvie was especially pleased.

'Look, it winds like a silver thread!' she cried.

WARPING MINOR WAS BUILT ON THE RIVER bank. It was a town full of weavers and Grimwade stopped the wagon in front of the first workshop in the main street. He and Lovegrove went inside and asked after Braid. At the mention of her name all the looms fell silent and the people looked up. A man came forward from the back of the shop carrying a small bolt of sackcloth.

'Friends of hers, are you?' he asked suspiciously.

Grimwade told him that they didn't know Braid but they wanted to talk to her.

'Well, you're the only ones who do,' he said. 'She's the cause of it all, you know.'

'The cause of what?' Lovegrove asked.

'The shortage. We'll be out of thread in another month. After that, there'll be no more cloth woven in this town.'

'Can you tell us where to find her?'

'No,' he said. 'I don't even want to say her name. The Weft brothers might help you. They're further on in Warping Major.'

THE TROUPE FOLLOWED THE RIVER TO the next town. It was bigger than Warping Minor but it was half empty. Dead trees lined the street and the remnants of a threadbare flag hung in front of the town hall.

The Weft brothers' workshop looked as if it had once been a large concern but had fallen into disrepair. Sylvie looked up and read the sign above the door.

The brothers were tall and thin. They were sitting in front of their shop idly playing with a yo-yo.

'It will…it won't…it will…it won't…' they said, as the yo-yo went up and down. They didn't seem to notice the troupe until the string broke and the reel rolled towards the wagon.

'It won't!' one brother said to the other. 'See? No thread will hold, not even string!' He stood up and went after the reel.

World's Finest Weavers
WEFT BROTHERS
SILKS SATINS BROCADES AND ORGANZA

When Lovegrove asked after Braid the men shook their heads sadly.

'She was the finest spinner in the valley,' the younger brother said. 'But look what she's done. See these trees?' He pointed into the dead branches overhead. 'Mulberry trees. All dead now, and the silkworms have dried up in their cocoons.'

'See those fields?' The other man waved towards the river. 'Last year those river flats were blue with flax. Now nothing will grow there.'

'It's worse further up the valley. And to think I once dreamed of working up there with the master weavers. There's no chance of that now.'

'There's nothing for us to do,' the older brother said. 'We've run out of thread and we've reached the end of our tether. We're ruined.' He put the reel in his pocket.

'Is Braid here?' Lovegrove asked.

'Further up,' the man sighed. 'If she's still around she'll be at Spindle Reach, on the far side of Loom. In the old days you had to be invited. Up there they made the really special fabrics.' The brothers exchanged glances and fell silent.

'What do they make back in Warping Minor?' Sylvie wanted to know.

'Coarse cloth.' The older brother flicked a strand of long hair from his eyes. 'Burlap, bunting and sacking. The further up the valley you go, the finer the weave.'

❧

THE WIDE TWINE VALLEY CLOSED IN AS the troupe travelled on. The river flats disappeared and soon the river was rushing beside them, fast and deep. By late afternoon Loom could be seen towering in the distance. The buildings were tall and narrow and they were perched on the edge of a cliff as if they were vying for the view. Some sort of large wheel contraption was behind them and a waterfall tumbled into the valley below. From the road it looked like a tress of long white hair.

The way grew steep and soon the troupe had to leave the wagon behind. Shoestring looked to the seatbox where May had stored his rope.

'Leave it,' she said. 'Grimwade will look after it.'

Grimwade unhitched Haul, then loaded Ace with a stack of blankets.

'In case you need to spend the night up there,' he said. 'I'll stay here and set up camp.'

Sylvie led the way up the track and Ace followed her. Shoestring hesitated for a moment, torn between staying with his rope and going after his gloves.

'This is a waste of time!' He spat the words out then headed up the path. Lobe and the rest of the troupe brought up the rear.

The track climbed steeply. Before long it was no wider than a footpath. It was wet and slippery and May had to keep stopping for rests. Even Lovegrove, with her long legs and sensible shoes, was struggling.

'Sylvie, is this really necessary?' May panted. 'This Braid woman may be of no use whatsoever, even if we find her.'

'That's true,' little Sylvie replied calmly, 'but she's all we've got to go on. Lean on me, May. I'll help you.'

The air was cold and damp and soon the path had a sheer drop on one side and a rock wall on the other. May glanced over the edge and saw the shattered remains of a cable car far below.

'I don't like this at all,' she gasped.

Shoestring could have helped May but instead he dawdled behind Ace, reaching out every now and then to touch the violin case.

The sun was going down by the time the troupe reached a set of steps that were cut into the rock. Nobody had used them for a long time. They were green with moss and there was a rickety railing beside them made of twigs bound together with vine.

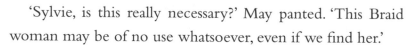

May didn't want to
trust the railing with her
weight. She leaned against
the rock wall and heaved
herself up one step at a time.
The Dittos stopped arguing in
order to save their breath and
for a while Shoestring paid
attention to where he put his
feet instead of watching the
violin case.

When May reached the
top of the steps a blast of wind
hit her with such force that
she almost lost her balance. She
struggled over a footbridge that
crossed the waterfall, then sat
down on the ground. Her legs were
shaking and she didn't dare look back,
although the view was breathtaking.

'That's it,' she said. 'No further
today. We'll stay the night up
here.'

One glance at the town
of Loom made her change
her mind.

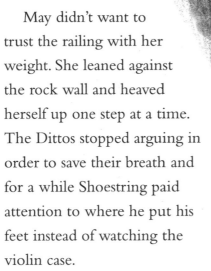

If Warping Major had been a big and busy place, Loom must have once been grand. Now the doors hung from their hinges and shutters were swinging in the wind. The streets were littered with broken looms and bits of torn fabric were being blown about like tumbleweed. The place was deserted, and apart from the banging shutters and the flapping of loose timbers, there was no sound except for the howling of the wind.

Lovegrove pointed across the road to a row of buildings. The first one had no front door. 'Let's shelter in there.' She had to shout above the wind to be heard.

The buildings were four storeys high and they had huge wooden pillars at the front that were carved to look like rope. There were pigeons nesting inside and when Lovegrove approached the open door they streamed from a top window like smoke.

Inside, the building was vast. The ceiling disappeared in darkness and on the walls hung the remnants of long tapestries that billowed in the wind. The floor was covered with feathers and bird droppings.

More birds rose from the centre of the hall, revealing the ancient loom on which they had been sitting. It was splattered with white mess and looked as if it hadn't been used for years. A piece of weaving was still on the frame but all the threads were broken. A feather caught in Sylvie's hair. She held it up and examined it.

'*Columba livia domestica*,' she said. 'Rock doves. Volume XX, page 843. This is an ideal habitat for them.'

Ace found the front door lying on the floor and, when he wedged it back in place, the howl of the wind was replaced by the gentle cooing of thousands of pigeons still roosting in the roof above. It was as if some great tragedy had happened and the birds were trying to soothe themselves with soft murmuring voices.

# CHAPTER TWENTY-TWO

# THE LADIES OF LOOM

**P**IGEONS AREN'T THE BRIGHTEST OF BIRDS. They all speak at once and they seem to only know a few words. The flock at Loom had a particularly limited vocabulary. I sat on May's shoulder and listened to them cooing. 'Woe, woe, woe,' they said over and over again. I felt like giving those featherbrains a piece of advice — 'If you keep saying 'woe', things will never get any better' — but of course I had no voice with which to impart this wisdom. I was relieved when one of their number came up with a different call.

'Twill,' I heard. 'Twill, twill, twill.'

The bird who made that sound was not in the lofty spaces above our heads but in a further room. I flew ahead to investigate and found myself in a parlour furnished with low tables and dilapidated cane chairs. I perched on the remains of a couch and looked about. There was a blackened fireplace and the picture on the wall above it showed four women standing next to a loom like the one I'd just seen. The image appeared to depict this house, but it must have been done a long time ago because the couch was new and covered in rich fabric and the windows were hung with lavish curtains. There were woven rugs on the floor and bright cushions on the chairs. The picture hung crookedly and every now and then the breeze lifted it and made it knock against the wall.

There were two pairs of doors in the room; the first was closed and rattling in the wind and the second opened onto a little balcony.

'Twill, twill!' The cry was coming from outside.

I flew to the window and looked out. The balcony was curved and it was edged with a low wall of woven birch sticks, which gave it the appearance of a nest. In that nest were the strangest chicks I'd ever seen.

For a moment I thought I was seeing some sort of monstrous hatchlings, but when they spoke I realised they were elderly ladies disadvantaged by the lack of a wardrobe. One was about May's age, the others were older. Two of them wore feather caps and the third, who was truly ancient, had a head that was bald as a coot.

'There's nobody about.' I heard May's voice from the hall. 'What a place! It's more like a pigeon loft than a house.'

'It could be a dovecote,' Sylvie replied, 'except for the loom.'

Startled by the voices, the women turned their heads and stared through the open doorway with vague, unfocused eyes. May let out a gasp. I could see what she was thinking: what on earth had happened to their clothes?

The women were shocked at the unexpected intrusion and May apologised. The oldest lady put her hands over her face before recovering her composure. 'Are you alone or with the flock?' she asked in a soft, crooning voice. She corrected herself. 'I mean with others,' she said. 'We haven't had visitors for so long we've forgotten who we are.'

'There's a few of us,' May replied. 'My name is May, Queen of Hearts.'

She stretched out her hand but the old lady ignored it and instead felt May's dress, running the fabric through her fingers.

'This reminds me of Cloud Chintz,' she cooed. 'A cloth we used to make. I think it's from the plains south of Cadenza city.' Then she examined May's feather boa.

'Do you keep pigeons, Mrs Heart?' she asked, staring at the space above May's head.

'I have a macaw who moults twice a year. The feathers came from her.'

I flew to May's shoulder, which was a mistake because the old woman began riffling through my plumage.

'Is the bird black?' she asked.

'Black with golden eye rings,' May replied. 'And her belly feathers are pink.'

'A striking combination,' the woman trilled.

At that point, Ace and the others appeared. A little shriek came from the twins and Lobe's mouth fell open.

'Birds?' KidGlovz asked.

Hugo began barking wildly until Lovegrove silenced him.

'Don't be alarmed,' May said. 'These ladies are…' She seemed to be searching for a way to describe their predicament when the oldest woman stood up and introduced herself.

'My name's Peg and this is my daughter, Fray, and my granddaughter, Twill. We are the Ladies of Loom. Excuse the feathers. We had to make do.'

Ace and Lobe hung back. I could see they thought their best bet would be to stay out of the way. But Lovegrove came forward. 'I'm Madame Lovegrove, and this is KidGlovz.'

The old lady reached out and grasped the front of Lovegrove's jacket.

'Cadenza tweed!' she crowed. 'A sturdy cloth and true. Quite hard wearing. But up here you'll only get three days out of it.' Her hand moved to Kid's shirt. 'Fullbright cotton,' she declared. 'Feel it, Fray.'

Her daughter reached for Kid's shirt and felt the weave.

'It's thin already. It won't last the evening.'

Sylvie had been watching from the doorway. She looked at the picture on the wall then back at the old women.

'Are you the master weavers?' she asked.

'Not anymore,' Fray sighed. 'We don't weave now. Our threads aren't strong enough.'

The three ladies lowered their heads, which was a relief because it meant I didn't have to see their strange eyes.

'What's gone is gone,' Peg crooned, scratching a bare patch on her elbow.

'Don't pick, Mother. You'll ruin your fluff,' Fray muttered softly.

I looked at the old lady's arm and saw that the skin was covered in dried mud. I realised that was how they had stuck on their feathers – they must have pressed them into the mud when it was wet.

'We made wonderful cloth in our day, didn't we?' Peg clasped her hands together, either in despair or to stop herself scratching. 'We made fabric that no one else could make and people came to us from all over the world.'

'When did you stop?' Sylvie asked.

'Not so long ago,' Fray sighed. 'But time is different here.'

The other women nodded and hummed their agreement in voices that sounded like pigeons.

'Did you come by the thousand steps?' Twill enquired, without looking up.

May told her we did and the three ladies made clicking sounds in the backs of their throats.

'We're sorry you had to walk. We used to have a cable car and pulley system.' Fray's hands fluttered around her face. 'But that's all gone now.'

'The cord broke,' her mother explained. 'It was one of the first things to go.'

'No strands up here will hold,' Fray sighed. 'Not ropes,

cables, cord, twine or yarn. Everything breaks. Still, it's nice to have visitors and feel your fabric.'

'While it lasts,' Twill added. 'You'll all be sky-clad in three days. Who else is here? Are there more of you?'

When May introduced the Ditto Twins, Fray touched the hems of their dresses and declared that they were both cut from the same cloth.

'No we're not,' Violet protested. 'I'm nothing like her.'

Peg felt the fabric of Lobe's shirt. 'Workweave from the west. This strong cloth will last four days,' she said.

Twill gave a little cry of surprise when she touched Hugo. 'Such long wiry hair! We had hair once.'

'But all the strands broke and then it fell out,' Fray said. 'Under our caps our heads are shiny and bald as new-laid eggs.'

'But we're forgetting ourselves!' Peg suddenly grew chirpy. 'Ladies, we have guests. They need refreshments. Twill, fetch the giving cloth!'

Twill felt her way past Lovegrove and the others as she hurried from the balcony. Her feet made scuffing sounds on the wooden floor. I heard her climbing some stairs and then coming down again. She returned with a small piece of blue cloth.

'This is lasting longer than most,' she explained. 'But it's not what it once was.'

She spread the cloth on a low cane table. It was thin and

faded and looked more like a cleaning rag than a tablecloth, but the ladies smiled proudly.

'One, two, three,' Peg counted them in, and they began singing in high warbly voices. *'A pot of tea. Cake and bread. Cheese and biscuits. Cloth, be spread!'*

*How pitiful*, I thought. The poor old things might know their fabrics but they'd been alone up here for so long that they'd taken leave of their senses.

I was glad I couldn't speak aloud because I would have had to eat my words — suddenly the little table was spread with teapot, cups, cake and bread, cheese and biscuits. The teapot had a feather cosy and Peg plucked it off the pot and put it on her head. 'That's better,' she said. 'Pour the tea before it gets cold.'

Fray filled the cups and invited everyone to eat. Nobody objected when I landed on the table and helped myself.

The youngest old lady, Twill, apologised for the fact that the cloth could not offer more. 'It's hardly working,' she told us. 'Once it would have provided a grand feast. Now we're lucky to get cheese and biscuits.'

'People used to come here for the giving cloth. It was one of our special weaves.' Peg looked past May with her cloudy eyes. 'Why have you come to us?' she asked.

'We're looking for someone called Braid.'

The Ladies of Loom sighed.

'Braid is Twill's daughter,' Peg said. 'She was a brilliant weaver and the very best spinner we had. She had the gift even as a baby. She would notice the spiders' webs and before she could walk, she crawled to the Twixt and collected fraz from the tree bark. She rolled it between her fingers, studying the length of the fibre.

'By the time she was five she had made a shimmering fabric that was as long as the waterfall and so fine it could fit in a matchbox. And by the time she was ten she knew all the weaves — the giving cloth, windweave, the copy cloth and the others. She even invented ones of her own.'

'She invented the cloaking cloth,' Fray cooed. 'It was so fine you couldn't see it and it hid whatever was behind it.'

'But she made a mistake,' Twill sighed.

The three women fell silent.

'Woe, woe, woe,' came the sound of the pigeons from inside the house.

'What sort of mistake?' Sylvie asked.

'She'll tell you about it,' Twill said quietly.

'Is Braid here?' May asked.

'She's up at Spindle Reach,' Twill replied. 'Poor Braid. She had no idea of the ruin she would cause.'

'But we forgive her.' Peg bit into a biscuit and the crumbs fell onto her lap, catching in her feathers on the way down. 'We would have done the same at her age.'

'But she won't forgive herself,' Twill said.

'Where's Spindle Reach?' May asked. 'Can you show us?'

The Ladies of Loom led us through their great draughty house. As they entered the hall, dozens of pigeons flew down and landed on their heads and shoulders.

'The birds have been a great comfort to us,' Peg muttered.

Ace removed the door and she led us out onto the street. 'If you hurry you'll be there before it's dark.' She gestured to the mountains beyond Loom.

We followed the Ladies of Loom up the main street and when we reached the end of the town Peg pointed towards a copse of spindly alpine trees.

'That's the Twixt,' she said. 'A path goes through there, then it goes on past the lakes. It leads to Spindle Reach.'

The trunks of the trees were low and twisted and the silver boughs grew through each other, all heading in the same direction, leaning out of the wind.

'Can you see a peak, further on?' Peg asked. 'That's the Twirl. If you reach there you'll know you've gone too far.'

In the distance I could see a rocky outcrop, the top of which was lost in swirling cloud. It made me feel dizzy just to look at it.

May thanked the ladies for their help. 'Will you be able to find your way back to your house?' she asked.

'The birds will show us,' Peg replied. 'They always know their way home.'

We passed the Twixt and headed across a plateau dotted with tiny lakes.

We're getting further and further away from the festival. I've got to get my gloves!

# CHAPTER TWENTY-THREE

# SPINDLE REACH

THERE WAS NO SHELTER BEYOND THE Twixt. The wind was strong and bitterly cold. It blasted down from the peaks and the smaller members of the troupe had

'Tween Twixt and Twirl and kith and kin...?

trouble staying upright. Low woody shrubs gripped the earth with claw-like roots, their tiny leaves trembling with each gust. The path wound its way between mountain lakes and everyone was soon drenched with the spray the wind picked up as it whipped across the water. Ace was the first to notice that his clothing was getting thin.

'That cold wind's blowing straight through my felt jacket.' He took one of the blankets he was carrying and wrapped it around himself.

Soon after that, Kid's trousers wore through at the knee and a rent appeared in Lovegrove's jacket. May tied her boa around her dress to try and hold it together, but the fabric was falling apart. Ace handed her a blanket to wear.

It was almost dark by the time the troupe saw Spindle Reach in the distance, and by then everyone was wrapped in blankets. Soon even the blankets were getting thin.

'I can't understand it,' Lovegrove said. 'They're thick woollen blankets. They should last for years, but they're getting more threadbare by the minute.'

Spindle Reach was a desolate little place. From a distance it looked like a pile of boulders stacked on a hilltop, but as the troupe drew closer they realised the boulders were little round stone huts. The wind died down as they approached and a twist of smoke rose from one of the domed roofs.

The troupe heard Braid before they saw her. She was chanting the rhyme that they now all knew by heart.

When they knocked on the door the sound abruptly stopped. They waited, but nobody came, so Sylvie pushed the door open and peeped inside. Braid sat by a small fire pit, staring into the coals. She looked different from the way she had appeared in Mot's painting. She was older and thinner and her hair had mostly fallen out. The patches that remained hung in broken strands. She wore a coat of plaited grass and in her hands she held a broken spindle.

'Come in. Warm yourselves.' She spoke without looking up, and when the visitors entered her hut she barely glanced at them. 'Spindle Reach was once the home of many fine spinners but now they're all gone. I'm the only one left.'

She pulled a thin blue rag from inside her coat and laid it on the bare floor of the hut. Then she muttered the same words the Ladies of Loom had sung, but all her giving cloth produced was a handful of breadcrumbs. She sighed and shook them into the fire.

She looked so small and frail that Lobe put a blanket over her shoulders.

'It's no use,' she said. 'It will fall apart by morning. It's all my fault.'

'What do you mean?' May asked.

The troupe sat down in the tiny hut and Braid told her story.

'I was the master spinner,' she said. 'I had a magical gift. I could spin straw into gold, night into day, the past into the future. There was nothing I couldn't spin. But I did the wrong thing and this is the result.'

She pulled out a strand of her hair and when it fell apart in her fingers, she put her head in her hands.

'Tell us what happened.' May gently put her hand on Braid's arm.

'It was pride. She said I couldn't do it and I wanted to prove her wrong.'

'Who?' May asked.

'I don't know her name. She was a powerful woman. Her henchmen wore stones on their fists, but it wasn't fear that made me do as she asked. It was the challenge.'

Braid took a stick and poked the coals.

'She said she'd pay me, of course. She offered me a jewel the size of a fist, but I don't care for such things.

'She arrived at dawn and spun me some tale that had no truth in it. She said her son was dead and she wanted to stitch him a present using a special thread, a thread that would last longer than memory, a thread that could never be broken.

'She dared me to try and make such a thread and when I hesitated, she said I couldn't do it.'

Braid sighed. She seemed to be talking to herself.

'So I closed my eyes and tried to feel the way of it, the twist, the turn, what fibre I would use, which words

I'd spin to fix the strands, and
when I looked up the sun was shining
through the diamond, dividing the
light into coloured rays. I had never
seen anything more beautiful.'

Braid lifted her head for the
first time. Her eyes were bright
and clear.

'You see, I'm different from the other women in my family,' she said. 'I can see, and looks can be deceptive. When I saw the light from the stone I knew I could make that thread. I plucked a silver hair from the old woman's head and plied it with the coloured rays. But as soon as the job was finished I wished I hadn't done it. I don't know why that woman wanted the thread but it can't have been for any good purpose, because since then no thread will hold. Even the spiders' webs break.'

'We know why she wanted it,' May said.

'I'm so sorry.' Braid hung her head again. 'I'm sorry for the ruin I've caused. But why have you come here?'

'We thought you might be able to help us,' May told her.

'What can I do? What's done is done.'

'Maybe not,' said Sylvie. 'Maybe you could undo what's done.'

Braid looked at Sylvie, noticing her for the first time. 'I don't understand.'

'Maybe you could unply the thread,' Sylvie went on. 'Undo the words, unspin the yarn. Is it possible?'

Braid didn't answer. She was thinking of the chant, of the words she had used to fix the thread. She was wondering if they could be changed.

*'Tween Twixt and Twirl and kith and kin*
*Unsplit the light, unspin … unspin …?*

'I don't know…' she said. 'The damage is already done.'

'I would like my memory back,' Kid said. 'I would like to recognise my friends and play music again.'

Lovegrove took his hand. 'Please help us, Braid.'

'Perhaps I could try,' Braid said doubtfully. 'I could turn the whorl the wrong way. But I would need to have the thread in the first place. I would need to hold it.'

'We have it.' Ace pointed over his shoulder. 'The gloves are right here in this violin case.'

'All right, I'll try,' Braid decided. 'At dawn tomorrow.'

*Those gloves are mine*, Shoestring thought. *They're mine and no one else is getting them.*

AS THE TROUPE SETTLED DOWN TO SLEEP by the fire, Shoestring told May he was going outside to stay in one of the empty huts.

'No, Shoe. Stay here.'

'Let him go,' Ace said. 'He can't do any harm.'

Shoestring stepped outside. He was sick of May watching him and worrying about him. He was sick of them all, and sick of this useless journey. He noticed the moon was full again. How many days had passed, he wondered, since he'd last worn the gloves. It felt like months. How he missed them! He closed his eyes for a second and felt the moonlight on his eyelids.

'It's not right,' he muttered. 'May and Ace have stolen my gloves and now they want to hand them over to a stranger.'

There was a piece of wood lying on the ground near his feet. It might have been a bit of broken loom or the shaft of a large spindle. Shoestring picked it up. He felt the weight of it in his hand and decided it would do the job. Instead of going into one of the empty huts, he crept around the back of Braid's place and waited until the troupe had gone to sleep.

I KNEW SHOESTRING WAS HATCHING A PLAN. You'd have to be dead as a dodo not to notice. I think that's why I couldn't sleep. I don't like to remember that night. I saw Shoe come into the hut and our eyes met, the intelligent gold-rimmed eyes of a Fabulous Macaw and the predatory eyes of a different species altogether – the eyes of a hunter, a masked owl. Then I knew nothing until I woke with my head thumping so hard there might have been some great thought inside it trying to get out.

May was hovering above me, moving in and out of focus as if she couldn't decide exactly what she was – a cloud, a bird or a woman wearing feathers. She was trying to speak to me but her words frayed at the edges and floated away before I could make sense of them. Finally she decided on her shape and the words became clearer.

'My old friend – thank goodness you're all right!'

She picked me up and placed me carefully on her shoulder, which was covered with the tattered remains of a blanket. From there I could see the others bending over Ace. The violin case was gone and he lay very still. 'A lump the size of an egg,' Lobe said, feeling the back of Ace's head. 'He's lucky to be alive.'

Ace groaned as they helped him sit up. 'We'll follow the boy,' he mumbled. 'He can't have gone far.' Ace tried to stand but he fell back.

'Rest, Ace,' Lobe said. 'We'll follow him in the morning.'

'I can't believe this has happened,' May cried, taking her cards from what was left of the bodice of her dress and shuffling them anxiously. 'Poor Ace. Poor Shoestring. My poor boys.' She dealt a card from the top of the pack and stared at it in horror.

Even May, who knew so little about the cards, could recognise The Abyss.

SHOESTRING RAN FROM SPINDLE REACH. He knew he'd run faster if the gloves were on his hands but he didn't want to risk stopping until he found a safe place to put them on. When he reached an outcrop of rocks on a rise just before the Twixt, he paused. From there he could see if he was being followed. He undid the belt and smashed the violin case open on a boulder. The gloves assembled themselves immediately, throwing a shadow on the face of the rock.

'We must hurry to the festival,' the shadow said. 'We don't want to miss the main event.'

Shoestring held out his hands and felt the surge of power as the gloves slipped onto them. He hurled the case away, then sprinted through the Twixt and down the main street of Loom before leaping across the footbridge and taking the steps that ran down the side of the waterfall two at a time.

He heard Grimwade snoring long before he reached the bottom. He decided he'd see if Lovegrove had something in her sewing kit he could use to pick the lock on the wagon seat but when he arrived he realised there was no need. He grabbed the padlock and tore it from the box. Then he slung his invisible rope over his shoulder and was gone before Grimwade was even out of his tent.

By the time Ace had recovered enough to stand up, Shoestring was running back along the Twine River road, halfway to Warping Major.

THE TROUPE LEFT BEFORE DAWN. SYLVIE led the way and Braid carried her spindle under her arm. They moved quickly through the ruined village. Soon they saw the broken violin case floating in the lake near the Twixt. Sylvie wished they had time to retrieve it. They ran straight through the town of Loom and when they were almost at the footbridge, Sylvie paused.

'I have to ask the ladies something. I'll catch you up.'

'Give them a message from me,' Braid said, as she hurried past. 'Tell them I'm going to try and reverse what I have done.'

Sylvie went into the house as the rest of the troupe headed down the thousand steps.

'Can you really tell where a cloth is made just by feeling it?' she asked the weavers.

'We're experts. We know everything there is to know about fabric,' Peg told her.

Sylvie took off her belt and placed it in the old woman's hands. The others felt the cloth as well.

'This is lasting well,' Twill said. 'It's from the north. It's that rough linen they weave up near Fiddleback Mountain.'

'The embroidery thread might come from one of the ferny glades in the foothills,' Fray added. 'The stitchwork feels nicely done. Your mother must have been skilful.'

'My mother?' Sylvie asked, surprised.

'Or your father. Whoever did the fancywork.'

Twill went into a back room and returned with a small silver basket. As she took Sylvie through the draughty hall towards the front door, a pigeon landed inside it.

'Thank you, little one,' Twill said to it. 'It won't be for long.' She put a lid on the basket and handed it to Sylvie.

'Give this bird to my daughter,' she said. 'Tell her to send word.'

'Go now,' Peg said. 'Go and catch up with your friends.'

'Thank you!' Sylvie cried.

THE TROUPE WAS WAITING AT THE BOTTOM of the valley. Haul was hitched to the wagon and Grimwade had packed away his tent.

'I heard a crash and I was outside in a second,' he said, 'but Shoe was gone. His footprints headed back along the road. I didn't want to go after him without the rest of you.'

Grimwade urged Haul into a steady trot and they reached Warping Major by lunchtime. The Weft brothers were still in front of their workshop. When they saw Braid sitting on the wagon with a basket on her lap they raised their eyebrows. Grimwade slowed down. He was going to ask if they'd seen Shoestring but May told him to keep going.

'We know where he's heading,' she said grimly. 'The Festival of Marvels.'

# CHAPTER TWENTY-FOUR

# Hurry, Hurry Hurry!

'HEY, YOU'RE COMING AFTER ALL!' THE Great Alexis called out.

'Of course!' Shoestring ran past the man's wagon without stopping.

He didn't need Alexis now. He didn't need a lift or a map or directions. The gloves knew where they were going. They pointed off the road and he jumped a fence and ran across farmland. He wasn't sure how far he ran. The sun went down and when it rose again he was still running.

On the second night he reached a town with a railway station. The platform was crowded.

'Last train to the festival. All aboard!' the guard cried.

Shoestring pushed his way onto the train along with everyone else. There were performers in the crowd: jugglers, tumblers and a tattooed man in a turban who had a green and gold snake twisted around his arm.

'Are you a magician?' he asked Shoestring, looking at his gloves.

'No, I'm a tightrope walker. I'm Shoestring – The Boy Who Walks on Air.'

'There's a tightrope competition at the festival,' the snake man told him.

'I know,' Shoe said. 'I'm going to win it.'

The carriage was crowded but Shoestring found a window seat. He smiled at his reflection in the glass as the train left the station. In his mind he was already walking triumphantly along the rope.

Shoestring dozed. When he woke the train had stopped and everyone was getting out. He looked through the window and gaped in surprise.

'Mount Adamantine! It didn't say that on the invitation.'

He pressed his face against the glass, trying to ignore the knot that had suddenly formed in his stomach. *Snap out of it!* he told himself. His fingers clicked in front of his face. Had he done that or was it the gloves? The knot disappeared.

The station was completely different from the last time he'd seen it. The abandoned railway tracks were now lined with stalls, painted booths and sideshows. Crowds poured off the train and streamed up the path, sweeping Shoe along.

'Roll up. Roll up!' a spruiker cried. 'Winner takes all!'

'Is this the Festival of Marvels?' Shoestring asked him.

'No lad, this is the foothills of the festival. The festival is

up on the mountain. It's starting tomorrow afternoon. You'd better hurry. Entries are closing for the big events.'

Shoe ran through sideshow alley and passed under some flags that marked the start of the track up the mountain. The trail was packed with people heading towards the summit. He didn't take his place at the end of the line – instead, he ran up along the edge of the crowd, moving so quickly people barely saw him pass.

MAY HOPED WE WOULD CATCH UP WITH Shoestring by the time we reached Five-Ways Junction, but when we arrived there was no sign of him.

'I can't understand it,' she said. 'He's on foot and we're in the wagon. He can't be too far ahead. Are you recovered, Metropolis? Would you mind having a look from the air?'

My head was still aching from the blow the night before. Maybe I was addled, because instead of flying low and searching for Shoestring among the crowds that streamed along the Tuffa Road, I caught a thermal and circled high above the traffic.

A bird's-eye view can be exhilarating, but sometimes a macaw can see too much. The crowds were heading towards a mountain – a mountain that looked as if the top had been cut off and the land beneath scooped out to form a hollow. People swarmed over the rim and they were coming from all

directions. I could see a settlement in the dip and around
it were thousands of tents. There was a small open space in
the centre. Black, it was, like the pupil of an eye. I thought
it might have been a lake. Beyond the tents was a building
surrounded by a wall.

I swooped down for a closer look and the shock at what I saw
almost stopped my heart. My flight feathers quivered. My
mind went blank and, had not instinct intervened with a swift
upstroke followed by a down, I would have slid into a tailspin
that could have been the end of me.

Luckily, nothing crossed my flight path on the way back to May — if any bird had strayed in front of me, no matter what size or species, I would have knocked it from the air.

May was full of concern. 'You're shaking, Metropolis. What is it?'

When I got my breath back and my heart's rhythm had settled to a fast tap dance, I hopped from May's shoulder to the atlas Sylvie had open on her lap.

Most macaws have four toes on each foot — two pointing forward and two pointing back — but the Fabulous Macaw has five, and the fifth one has a hooked talon that's sharp as her mind and possibly just as dexterous. It was my fifth talon that I used to scrabble through the atlas in search of the index at the back and if pages were torn to shreds as I did so, it couldn't be helped — you can't make an omelette unless you crack a few eggs. When I reached the first page of the index, I stabbed my beak down so hard I punctured the back cover. Then, with an apologetic glance at Sylvie, I lifted my head and ran my beak carefully down the list until I reached *Adamantine, Mount*.

'I thought as much!' May cried. 'I don't want to go back to that place. I vowed to leave it behind me.'

*Good*, I thought. *Let's go home to Cadenza. Tell Grimwade to turn the cart around. Let's forget about Shoestring and the festival. Let's forget about everything.*

Already I could see my happy life at the Luck Palace returning. I would fly between the tables in the gaming room,

I would hang from the chandelier and spy on the card games, I would land on Lobe's shoulder and ask him to fill me in on everything he'd heard. Then I remembered that Lobe had lost his splendid hearing just as I had lost my voice. I looked at KidGlovz, who was reading the book with his name on the front, trying to recall his past. Then I looked at Braid. She was staring hopefully at the road ahead as if it promised a future that she had thought lost.

May sighed. 'I don't want to go, but I must.'

When Grimwade steered the wagon along the Tuffa Road I put my head under my wing. I had the uneasy feeling that once we reached Mount Adamantine all our chickens would come home to roost. The fact that neither May nor I had ever laid an egg did nothing to reassure me.

# PART SIX

# CHAPTER TWENTY-FIVE

# THE FESTIVAL OF MARVELS

SHOESTRING RAN OVER THE RIM OF THE mountain and headed down into a sea of tents and people.

'Where do I enter the competition?' he asked.

The gloves pointed the way to the official stand and he was surprised to find his name was already on the board that listed the competitors. It was at the top.

### DEATH-DEFYING
### FAME & FORTUNE AWARD
#### ALL CONTESTANTS REGISTER HERE
SHOESTRING — THE BOY WHO WALKS ON AIR
THE GREAT ALEXIS — AIRWALKER EXTRAORDINAIRE
MR SPELTANI VERTIGO
THE ALTITUDINOUS TUMBLERS
MIKE THE KITE
HIGH-FLYING PHILLIPO

'I need to use my own rope,' he told the man behind the counter.

'No problem,' was the reply. 'Go and rig it up over the pit.'

The gloves led him to some scaffolding that had been erected at the edge of the mine. There was a platform above with a ladder leaning against it. As Shoestring began climbing he could feel the updraft lifting his hair. A big metal ring was bolted to the edge of the platform and Shoe looped his rope through it.

*I'd better tie it well*, he thought. *Double knots. Triple knots.*

'That's Shoestring!' someone yelled from below. 'He's the one who walks on air.'

'I've heard of him. He'll win for sure.'

The spectators on the ground weren't the only ones looking at Shoestring. In her tower, Mistress Adamantine adjusted the telescope and watched him fix his rope. She saw him descend the ladder then skirt the pit to a second platform that stood on the far side. Satisfied, she turned from the window and, retracting her telescope, sat down at a table and stared at the Eye of the Dragon.

'I'm going to break her heart, my darling,' she whispered. 'As she broke mine.'

**I** ADMIRE THE OSTRICH. SHE GROWS THE most luxuriant feathers of any bird I know. Her plumage can be used for hats and headdresses and her gorgeous wing feathers can make splendid fans. If she has a tendency to bury her head in the sand in times of trouble, who can blame her?

As we travelled to the festival I kept my head tucked firmly beneath my wing, glad my feathers were muffling the sounds around me. I didn't hear May fretting about Shoestring, or Ace commenting how the weather was closing in. I heard nothing except my own raucous thoughts and, being a bird who knows her own mind, I decided to quieten them by travelling back to a time when I was safe, a time before May, before Marm, before my first owner stole me from the nest.

I let myself drift like mist into the deep green forest of the Archipelago. I went so far back, I wasn't even laid: soft-shelled and barely formed, I was a tiny moon travelling in the dark night of my mother. It was evening and she was one of many. Macaws covered the treetops like black foliage and, as they settled for the night and my mother closed her eyes, I entered the mind of the flock, a vast and silent place, a timeless realm in which a bird can find true peace if she's not interrupted.

'Metropolis! Wake up. We're here!'

It was May. Sometimes that woman has a voice on her like a galah.

I peeped out through the tips of my flight feathers. Grimwade had parked the wagon near a lake. It was a quiet spot and there was no sign of a festival.

*This can't be it*, I thought, and I was right. I looked up and saw Mount Adamantine in the distance. The sky behind it was iron grey, the same colour as my beak. I usually like iron grey but on that sky it looked heavy and threatening. A line of people were trailing up the mountain. They could have been ants.

'Come on,' May said. 'Let's go before it rains.'

'How will you find him?' Grimwade stared at the mountain. 'There are thousands heading up there.'

'One step at a time,' Sylvie said. 'First we have to get there.'

We followed a track that led to the main road. Like us, everyone was parking their wagons and continuing on foot. People stared as we joined the throng. We must have looked a sorry band, Braid in her grass coat and the rest of us dressed in rags and threadbare blankets. I was the only one who looked presentable. My eyes shone and my feathers were sleek and glossy. When someone made a snide remark in May's direction I gave them a killing look, then puffed out my breast and held my head high. May and I might not always agree, but we're birds of a feather and I won't have anybody put her down.

'Metropolis, it doesn't matter,' she said. 'We'll get some new clothes soon.'

The sky darkened and thunder rumbled in the distance. It began to rain and the crowd surged forward. Soon we came upon a scattering of buildings. One of them was a railway station. People poured over the platform and onto the railway tracks. The place was unrecognisable and the noise was deafening. Everyone seemed to be shouting at once.

'Every player wins a prize!'

'Step right up and knock 'em down!'

'Test your skill and try your luck!'

A woman spun a giant wheel with such force that the wind from it lifted my wings and almost blew me off May's shoulder. 'Is your number up?' she shrieked.

May found a tent selling clothing. The selection was poor: every item inside was black, and not the lustrous black of the Fabulous Macaw but a dull sort of black that absorbs light rather than reflects it. There were black shirts, black shawls and a rack of drab black dresses, the sort of clothes you wouldn't be seen dead in. The only frock that fitted May was a stiff number with a high collar and some sort of corsetry built into it. She came out of the tent looking like she was heading for a funeral. Braid preferred to stick with her grass coat.

Sylvie pointed through the crowd. 'Look!' she cried. 'A *Morelia spilota spilota*.'

We followed as she ran towards a tent with a sign that said COUNT ABDULLA THE SNAKE MAN. A fellow sat on the ground playing a flute. He had a huge snake draped over his shoulders. A snake that size could easily devour a macaw.

'It's also known as the diamond python,' Sylvie said.

There was a fire eater next to the snake man. He wore a dragon mask that was singed at the edges and had a blackened hole where the mouth should have been. He stood on a box and held a flaming torch.

'Hear the Legendary Flambé,' he cried. 'Tall tales and true, straight from the tongue of fire!'

He waited until a crowd gathered around him then began telling a story.

'There was once a one-eyed dragon. His belly was a forge and his breath...' The man paused and a small flame issued from the hole in his mask. 'His breath was fire!' The crowd cheered and the man took off his mask and licked his lips before continuing. 'That dragon was smouldering deep under the earth. His snoring made the mountain rumble...'

'Look out!' someone yelled. 'Here comes the ghost train!'

The crowds parted, leaping off the tracks. People scrambled over each other to get out of the way but May kept standing where she was. A great black steam train was bearing down on us. I don't know where it came from. May and I could have lost everything in one fell swoop had not Ace grabbed us and hauled us from the tracks.

The train shrieked past. It was driven by some pale-looking girls who put me in mind of the maids at the House of Diamonds. They were so thin you could see through them. Revellers hung from the windows of the carriages and screamed as the train careered past. It was gone in a flash. The fire eater seemed unconcerned; he was still telling his story.

'... and when the dragon found his eye, the mountain burst and blew sky high!' he yelled.

Whooooosh! A fountain of fire came from his mouth.

Everyone screamed and leapt back except a lady with a toasting fork who had the next stall. 'Barbecue drumsticks going cheap!' she yelled, as she held them into the flames. The crowd laughed but I didn't think it was funny. The sizzling smell turned my stomach and I know it turned May's as well. May never ate poultry out of respect for my feelings and she often said the only thing she'd ever pluck was her eyebrows.

We hurried on. Ahead was a carousel that was going much too fast. The horses were painted with flames and their manes and tails looked like fire. The children on their backs screamed and hung on for grim death.

'Boys and girls, line up for the ride of your life!' a man yelled.

'I don't like this place,' I heard KidGlovz say.

'It's a nightmare,' Sylvie agreed.

Beyond the carousel was a sight that made me shudder. It was a shooting gallery with black macaws instead of ducks.

Bang. Bang. Bang. The sound of the guns rang in my ears. May covered my eyes.

'Look, May.' Ace pointed ahead, then he changed his mind. 'No, don't look!' he cried, but it was too late. Next to the shooting gallery was a row of laughing clowns. Their mouths gaped and their heads turned from side to side. The game could have been amusing but the clowns wore turbans fastened with heart-shaped brooches and each one looked like May. She turned pale.

'Let's get out of here,' she gasped.

It seemed a long way to the end of sideshow alley. May broke into a run and I bounced up and down on her shoulder. I kept my eyes fixed straight ahead. I had seen enough and May had too. I barely registered Miss Lilly White's Odditorium and the eight-armed juggler who stood outside trying to entice people into her tent with cries of, 'Fabulous exhibits. Unbelievable anatomical wonders.' I closed my ears to spruikers calling for customers — 'Dare-devil rides. Big prizes. Not for the fainthearted!'

There were some flags ahead like the ones they have at the start of a race. We passed under them and left the sideshows behind.

The track up the mountain was long and steep. There had been snow but it was melting and the ground was slushy underfoot. To tell you the truth I don't know how May managed to walk that far. At the Luck Palace she bustled in and out of the gaming room and she probably made several trips a night up and down the stairs to Mr Goldfiend's shop, but I would never have described her as fit. Still, she'd managed the thousand steps to Loom and now she was proving herself stronger than I imagined, panting her way up Mount Adamantine. I was full of admiration for her and I was just dozing off to sleep thinking how plucky she was when she knocked me from my perch.

'Metropolis, will you pull your weight!' she gasped. 'Get off! It's hard enough without hauling a great stuffed turkey like you across the country!'

*How rude!* I thought as I got to my feet. I am a large and powerful bird, massively beaked and strong boned. I admit I am somewhat heavy in the undercarriage but can I be blamed for that? I found May's comment truly hurtful. I waited on the ground for some minutes and when nobody picked me up I flew to Lobe. Lobe was a gentleman. He knew how to treat a lady. He gave a little sigh as I landed on his shoulder.

I looked at May. I could see she was struggling. She was wet and bedraggled and that dress wasn't doing her any favours — it was difficult to walk in and the road was getting steeper with every step she took. Still, that was no excuse for treating me badly.

THE JOURNEY UP THE MOUNTAIN TOOK ALL night. It was dawn when we came over the top and gazed down on a vast plain covered with people.

'Look at that!' cried Daisy.

'Breathtaking!' Sylvie agreed.

'I've never seen so many people.'

'Not the people, the landscape,' Sylvie said. 'I believe it's a caldera — the basin of an extinct volcano.'

'How are we to find Shoestring in that crowd?' May asked. 'Metropolis, can you look for him?'

I tucked my head under Lobe's chin. I wasn't going to

help May. I'd need a full apology before I'd even look in her direction.

'Let's find the place where the performers go to register,' Sylvie suggested.

May led the way to the competitors' stand but Shoestring wasn't there.

'He's the odds-on favourite,' someone told her. 'He's tipped to win.' The official pointed to a board with Shoestring's name on it.

```
SHOESTRING........................................ 5 / 4
      - THE BOY WHO WALKS ON AIR -
THE GREAT ALEXIS............................... 5 / 1
      - AIRWALKER EXTRAORDINAIRE -
MR SPELTANI VERTIGO........................ 20 / 1
THE ALTITUDINOUS TUMBLERS................ 50 / 1
   MIKE THE KITE.................................100 / 1
HIGH-FLYING PHILLIPO..................... 500 / 1
```

'Do you want to place a bet?' the man asked.

May shook her head. She turned away and burst into tears. 'This will come to no good, I know it! We've got to find him.'

I hopped back on May's shoulder. Sometimes there's no point in bearing a grudge.

'Spread out, everyone,' she said. 'Let's meet back here in an hour.'

May and I headed down a lane of tents selling trinkets and food. It turned into a street that was part of the old settlement. May shuddered when we passed an ancient sign. 'NO BEGGARS, HAWKERS OR...' was all that you could read.

We came to some open ground around the pit. I flew above May's head and scanned the crowd. It was still raining and many people held umbrellas with WELCOME TO JUBILEE FESTIVAL written around the edges. Shoestring was no fool. He'd be hiding under an umbrella for sure. I flew back down to May.

As we wandered among the throng May lost track of time. One hour became two and two became three. She grew increasingly desperate.

'This is impossible, Metropolis,' she said. 'Maybe the others are having more luck.'

An announcement was shouted through a loudspeaker telling people that the event was about to begin. May became frantic and redoubled her efforts.

'Shoestring!' she cried. 'Shoe. Shoe!'

She knew it was hopeless, trying to find a boy who didn't want to be found in a crowd like that. Finally, she looked towards the tower.

'It's me she wants, Metropolis. I'm going to have to face her.'

My crest shot up and I stared at May with wide eyes. I could see she was at her wit's end — but had she lost her mind?

*No!* I thought. *May, don't!*

I left her shoulder and flapped in front of her face as she began walking towards the tower.

'Out of my way.' She swept me aside.

The rest of the crowd were heading in the opposite direction, so she had to force her way through.

'Hey, you're going the wrong way,' someone told her.

'Stand aside!' she cried.

I followed May to the House of Diamonds and watched as the guards seized her and took her inside, slamming the gate behind them. I could have followed. I could have flown over the wall and tried to help. But my courage failed. I turned back.

Did I mention the fact that I have a heart murmur? It's a condition I've had since I was chick and one that the Fabulous Macaw, being a sensitive bird, is prone to. My heart missed several beats and fluttered like a butterfly as May disappeared through the gate.

*Look after yourself, Metropolis,* I thought. *There's no point in both of us going down for the sake of that wretched boy.*

It took me ages to find a member of the troupe. Ace was waiting at the competitor's stand.

'Where's May?' he wanted to know.

I sat on his shoulder, hunched and dejected.

Lovegrove appeared. 'No sign of him?' she asked.

Ace shook his head. 'And now we've lost May as well.'

The Dittos showed up half an hour later.

'Nothing,' they said. 'He's been seen, but where he is now is anyone's guess.'

'He'll be hiding somewhere near the pit,' Lovegrove said. 'Keep looking.'

I STARED AT THE GROUND. I KNEW I SHOULDN'T have let May go alone. I could have protected her.

*I could still protect her*, I told myself. *Metropolis, be brave. You've got a beak. You've got claws…*

I thought of Mistress Adamantine — her claws were like talons and she was fierce as an eagle. What chance would I stand against her? She'd snatch me from the air and bite my head off. I put my head under my wing as Ace pushed his way through the crowd.

# CHAPTER TWENTY-SIX

# AN EYE FOR AN EYE

THE GUARDS ESCORTED MAY UP THE SPIRAL stairs and into the tower where Marm was waiting. She held a feather duster in her hand.

'Hello, May. I knew you would come,' she said. 'I've saved you a seat, a ringside seat.'

Two chairs were set up at a table, and on the table was Shoestring's photo. May gasped. It was the photo she kept on her mantelpiece and it was now in a diamond-studded frame. Next to it was the Eye of the Dragon.

'All the contestants will walk the pit.' Marm gestured towards the window with her duster. 'Some may make it across to the other side, but your boy won't. You see, May, it's an eye for an eye and a life for a life. You killed Jack Diamond and now you must pay the price.'

May picked up Shoestring's photo and her eyes filled with tears. 'But he's only a boy,' she pleaded. 'He's done nothing wrong, except for the things he did while he was wearing your gloves.'

'Oh, the gloves…' Marm waved the duster above her head as if she was whisking away a stray thought. 'Let's just say the gloves were the support act. Now it's time for the main event.'

She leaned across the table. 'Those gloves were a stroke of luck, May. They stole one of my stones – I think it was an amethyst. At first I blamed the guards. But then I learned that a wild pair of gloves was abroad on the night of each full moon. There had been sightings all over the country. One of my men claimed to have seen those gloves flying through the bars of my window. When they came a second time I can tell you I was waiting for them.'

Marm remembered that night. She'd laid some precious stones on a table much as a hunter might bait a trap. Above them hung a net, and she'd ordered her guards to stand on either side of the window and close the shutters as soon as the gloves arrived. When she pulled the trip-string the gloves were easily caught. They flapped wildly as her henchmen stuffed them into a gilded cage. The men covered the cage with fine wire mesh so the gloves couldn't escape, then Marm took the cage to her room and hung it above her bed.

'I felt they might be useful to me,' she told May, 'but I wasn't sure how. I'd heard of a fellow called Mot, an old hermit who could apparently dream the answer to any question he was asked. I decided I'd pay him a visit.'

Marm cast her mind back to that day. 'Why do you need the gloves?' the old fool had asked. What a cheek! She gave her henchmen a nod and they grabbed the hermit and held him up against the wall. 'I'll ask the questions and you give the answers,' she said.

She smiled at the thought and touched May's hand. 'He needed some persuasion... but my bodyguards can be very persuasive. It wasn't hard to replace the thread. I waited until the dark moon, and when the gloves went limp, I pulled out the old thread and replaced it with the new one I'd got from Braid. Then the gloves were mine! They were a pair of willing hands, and I had work to do!

'I could have ordered those gloves to strangle you in your bed, May, but that would have been too good for you. Instead, I created this marvellous festival.

'It took some planning, I can tell you. First, I had to steal your bird. Then I had the gloves pop a feather of hers into an envelope addressed to you. I made the invitations and advertised the festival throughout the land. I knew the boy would bring you here just as I knew the bird would bring the boy. I stole Metropolis's voice, you know.'

'You did? Why?'

Marm gave a satisfied laugh. 'The bird had too much to say for herself. I didn't want her giving the game away.'

May stared over Marm's shoulder and through the bars of the window. The rain had stopped and the sun was low in the sky. She could see the festival site in the distance. Crowds were swarming around the pit.

'All this is for you,' Marm said. 'Please sit down.'

May sat. She held Shoestring's photo in both hands.

'You can't save him, May,' Marm whispered, then suddenly she lashed out and knocked the frame to the floor.

'Yes, all this is for you,' she laughed. 'And it's also for me. I vowed I wouldn't die until I'd avenged my son's death. Today is my birthday, my diamond jubilee. I'm seventy-five. The festival will be a celebration.'

Marm took the monocle from her eye and extended it into a telescope. She handed it to May.

'I must go and open the competition. I'll leave you to watch in private.' She headed for the door.

'I didn't mean to kill Jack Diamond!' May cried. 'I was trying to protect Metropolis.'

Marm paused and looked over her shoulder. 'I've been waiting all my life for this moment. I'm too old to forgive.'

'Wait,' May cried. 'Let's play for him!'

'Play?' Marm raised an eyebrow.

'Cards,' May said, taking them from her bodice. 'Would you like a game?'

She began shuffling the pack. Her hands were shaking so much she dropped some cards on the floor.

*I've got to play for time*, she thought, as she picked them up. *Give the others a chance to find him.*

May was a good player. She'd never lost a game.

She looked Marm in the eye, challenging her. 'If I win, Shoestring lives. If you win, the competition goes ahead.'

Marm smiled and sat down at the table. 'All right,' she said. 'But they're not proper playing cards.'

She clapped her hands and a guard opened the door.

'Get some cards,' she ordered. 'Two sets.'

'What game will we play?' May asked. 'Broken Joker? Crazy Eights? Royal Flush?'

'I don't know those games. Let's play Snap.'

The game was fast and furious. Marm's eye was sharp but May's hands were quick. When May had won several rounds, Marm's eyes narrowed. She didn't like to lose. She put down her second-last card. It was a jack of diamonds. May put a queen of hearts on top of it. Marm also had a queen of hearts. She put it down then they both slammed their hand over the cards.

'Snap!' they cried.

May looked at Marm's bony hand with its diamond rings. It was on top of hers. May had clearly won.

But Marm leapt to her feet, screaming, 'You cheated!' May opened her mouth to protest, but abruptly Marm turned her head. She took a deep breath and stared out the window. Then she sat back down.

'Well, this has been an amusing little game, May,' she said. 'It's time for me to go.'

'But I won!'

'Nobody beats Mistress Adamantine.' Marm picked up her diamond and handed her telescope to May for a second time. 'Enjoy the show,' she said as she left the room, locking the door behind her.

The guards followed Marm as she swept down the stairs. When she reached the bottom she clapped her hands.

'Everyone must attend the festival,' she commanded.

May put her eye to the glass and watched Marm and her guards leaving the House of Diamonds. The sun was going down and their shadows stretched before them. The crowd parted to let them pass as they headed towards the mine.

May focused the telescope. There were high platforms on either side of the pit. She'd seen them before, but what she hadn't noticed was a third platform built out over the drop. A walkway led to it. The guards stood aside as Marm strode towards this platform.

May searched the crowd. Maybe the troupe had found

Shoestring and he was safe with them. Was it too much to hope for? She scanned a sea of umbrellas, catching sight of faces in the gaps, but none of them was familiar. Then she saw Daisy Ditto. The telescope was powerful — May could see the detail on Daisy's earring. KidGlovz was nearby but almost immediately he disappeared from view. May pulled back and saw that Madame Lovegrove was holding his hand and dragging him behind her as she ran. She was searching frantically.

May caught a glimpse of Ace, looking behind the food stalls. Metropolis sat on his shoulder with her head tucked under her wing. Beyond the food stalls was the open ground beside the mine. May panned across it to Marm, who was now standing on the platform at the end of the walkway. There were lights just under the rim of the pit and as the sun went down they grew brighter. They reminded May of stage lights, only there was no stage, just a black hole. Marm stood watching the sun, and when it had dipped behind the horizon she raised her hand, a signal for the spotlight. Suddenly her hair shone like silver and her skin was white as bone. She spread her arms and addressed the crowd.

'Welcome to the Diamond Jubilee Festival of Marvels. The first event will be spectacular, ladies and gentlemen — an event to end all events! The risk is great but so is the prize.'

There were gasps from the audience when she held up the red diamond.

'It gives me great pleasure to open the festival with the Death-Defying Fame and Fortune Award for the World's Leading Highwire Artist. Our first contestant is Shoestring – The Boy Who Walks on Air!'

May couldn't hear what Marm was saying but she heard a roar from the crowd. Then she saw Shoestring climbing the ladder to the platform on the far side of the pit. She adjusted Marm's eyeglass until he filled the lens. He was wearing the white gloves and he looked supremely confident.

# CHAPTER TWENTY-SEVEN

# BATTLE OF THE BIRDS

'THERE HE IS!' CRIED SYLVIE. SHE WAS standing with Braid and Lobe and the twins. Lobe ran towards the ladder and when he reached it he found Ace, Lovegrove and KidGlovz there as well.

'Stay back. You can't interfere with the competition,' the officials said.

Ace knocked them aside and yelled up at Shoestring.

'Get down. Shoestring, get down!'

'Go away. Leave me alone!' the boy answered. He had almost reached the platform.

Ace began climbing the ladder but he'd only stepped up a few rungs when one of Marm's henchmen appeared and pulled him back. Lovegrove and Lobe tried to help and in the struggle Metropolis was flung into the air.

May saw none of that. All she saw was Shoestring. He reached the platform and stepped onto the invisible rope, putting one foot carefully in front of the other. May held her breath. He did a little skip and the audience roared.

Shoestring smiled. His act had barely started and already he had the audience in his thrall. He did a cartwheel and a backflip, then he ran to the centre of the rope and paused, spreading his hands to receive the adulation of the crowd.

*Keep going*, May thought. Her heart was in her mouth. Shoestring was halfway across the abyss. *He's walked the rope a thousand times before*, she told herself. *He won't fall… he can't fall…*

At that moment the gloves left Shoestring's hands and flew towards the platform. They landed on the ring and began pulling at the knots. May put down the telescope and stood holding the bars of the window, tears streaming down her face.

'I can't look,' she said.

Shoestring stared in disbelief. 'What are you doing?' he cried. 'My gloves… my beautiful gloves…'

The troupe stared in horror.

'We're too late,' said Braid.

'Maybe not,' Sylvie muttered. She wasn't looking at the gloves or at Shoestring – she was looking at Metropolis, who had landed on a rung near the top of the ladder. 'Metropolis!' she yelled. 'Help!'

I LOOKED DOWN AT THE CROWD. SYLVIE WAS yelling at me and so was Braid.

'Help him! Save him!' they cried.

*Who? Me?* I thought.

They pointed above my head and foolishly I hopped up the last couple of rungs of the ladder to the platform, where I found myself just a few wing strokes from the gloves. They didn't see me. They were busy pulling something apart, something I couldn't see.

'The rope!' Sylvie yelled.

I realised what was happening. The fat fingers of the gloves were working at the knots. Shoestring was a long way out across the gap. His face was white with fright and he looked very young. He was standing perfectly still.

'Help!' He mouthed the word.

My beak began chattering and my wing tips trembled. 'Go on,' I told myself. 'You've got the equipment – talons to die for, a beak like a boltcutter. You might not be a match for Marm but maybe you could hold your own against the gloves, for a minute or two, for just as long as it takes Shoestring to get off the rope.'

Why wasn't he moving? The fool!

'Save him, Metropolis!' Ace shouted.

I looked down at Ace, then I looked towards the tower. I could just make out May standing at the barred window. She reminded me of myself when I was in the cage.

'Metropolis, do something!' Lobe yelled. Then I heard the shrill voices of the twins, one coming from the left of the platform and one from the right. Their cries met in the middle of my mind and dissolved whatever resistance I had left. I knew I had to act.

I flapped into the air and, without so much as a battle cry, I launched myself at the left glove, knocking it off the rope and onto the platform. It was solid and heavy, as if it had a hand inside it. We landed with a thud. The impact knocked the breath out of me and it must have done the same for the glove because it immediately went limp. I collected myself and flew at its partner. The right glove was no longer pulling at the rope. It lay palm-down across the ring and I realised whatever stunned one glove must stun the other as well.

'Good girl, Metropolis!' I heard Sylvie cry. But the gloves were only playing dead. At the sound of Sylvie's voice they came

together and within seconds I found a white bird hovering over me. It seemed to be twice my size and as it gathered height, preparing to attack, the suck of its mighty wingdrag almost lifted me from the platform. I knew I was in trouble.

They say discretion is the better part of valour — I hopped two steps to the ladder and, locking my claws around the top rung, I swung myself upside down under the platform moments before the gloves dived. In a blink their prey had disappeared and they had to back up hard not to hit the boards.

'Chicken!' someone yelled from below.

I felt my gall rise. As you probably know, the gall of the Fabulous Macaw is located next to her liver and beneath the awe-inspiring arch of her wishbone. No one was going to call me *chicken* when I'd put myself at risk trying to save a boy's life.

I left the cover of the platform and propelled myself upwards with all the strength I had. Altitude is everything in these situations.

'Go Metropolis!' I heard Lovegrove yell, or maybe it was Braid.

I knew I had the weight of the troupe behind me, and that, coupled with my own considerable weight, made me a force to be reckoned with. I could deploy myself like a missile. I flew high above the platform and when the gloves were in my sights, I plummeted towards them in a death-defying freefall.

The gloves were swift and cunning. I'd like to think my aerial skills were superior, but my opponent had the advantage of supernatural strength. Still, I had to believe that luck was on my side. I swooped in close with my beak open and I sideswiped the gloves, hooking my upper mandible in their fabric. I heard the cloth rip and when I looked back, one glove was flapping in the wind. It amazed me that they kept flying with only one wing.

The crowd cheered, egging me on.

'The thread, Metropolis,' Sylvie yelled. 'Get the thread!'

I swung out wide, then I lined up the gloves with the top of my beak.

'Go for the seam,' she cried.

I zeroed in on my target and when I was within stabbing distance I punctured the side seam and bit down with all my might. The thread was supple but stronger than wire. It was diamond-hard. Even a beak like mine couldn't bite through it. I pulled back, shaking my head from side to side, trying to tug it free. My opponent struggled from my grasp and retreated to the far side of the pit. I didn't get the thread but I had vanquished the enemy. The crowd roared. I landed back on the platform and turned to acknowledge the applause, raising my crest in a victory salute.

'Look out!' yelled the dual voices of Dittos.

The gloves had wheeled around and were coming at me so fast I didn't have time to take cover. With one wing slap

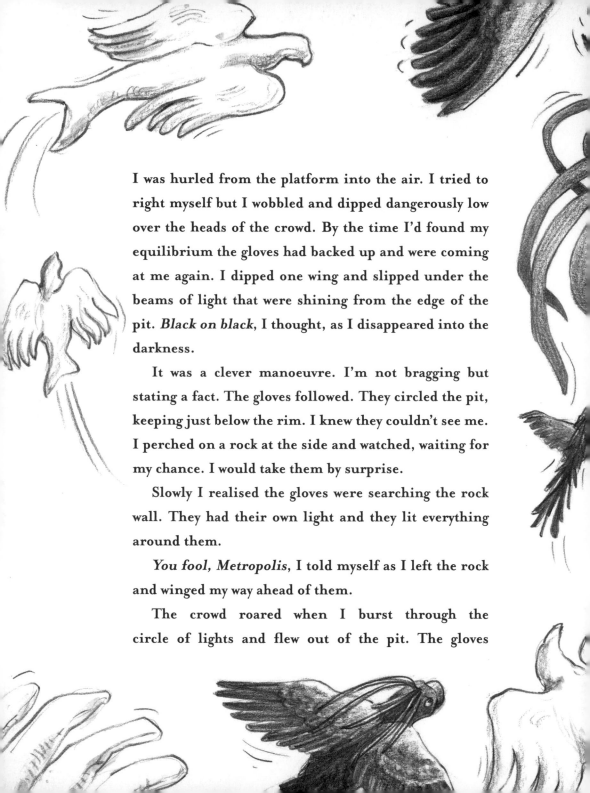

I was hurled from the platform into the air. I tried to right myself but I wobbled and dipped dangerously low over the heads of the crowd. By the time I'd found my equilibrium the gloves had backed up and were coming at me again. I dipped one wing and slipped under the beams of light that were shining from the edge of the pit. *Black on black*, I thought, as I disappeared into the darkness.

It was a clever manoeuvre. I'm not bragging but stating a fact. The gloves followed. They circled the pit, keeping just below the rim. I knew they couldn't see me. I perched on a rock at the side and watched, waiting for my chance. I would take them by surprise.

Slowly I realised the gloves were searching the rock wall. They had their own light and they lit everything around them.

*You fool, Metropolis*, I told myself as I left the rock and winged my way ahead of them.

The crowd roared when I burst through the circle of lights and flew out of the pit. The gloves

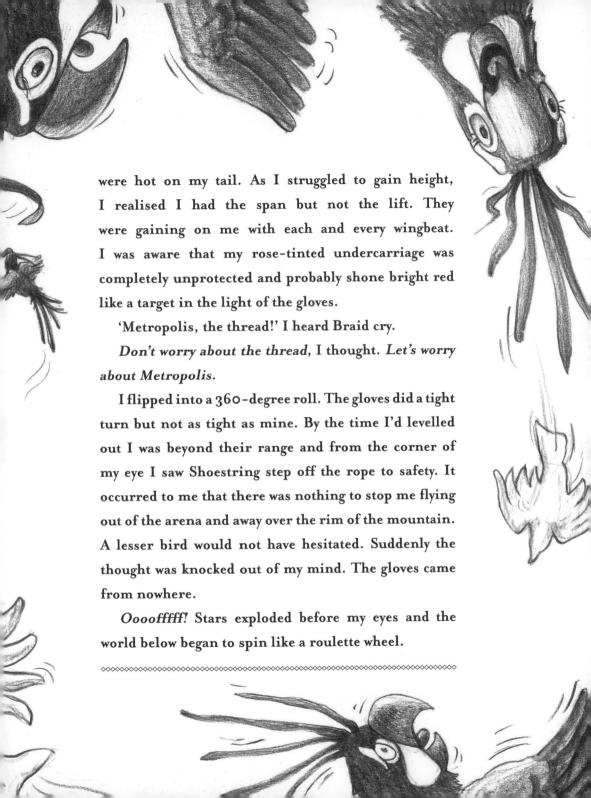

were hot on my tail. As I struggled to gain height, I realised I had the span but not the lift. They were gaining on me with each and every wingbeat. I was aware that my rose-tinted undercarriage was completely unprotected and probably shone bright red like a target in the light of the gloves.

'Metropolis, the thread!' I heard Braid cry.

*Don't worry about the thread*, I thought. *Let's worry about Metropolis.*

I flipped into a 360-degree roll. The gloves did a tight turn but not as tight as mine. By the time I'd levelled out I was beyond their range and from the corner of my eye I saw Shoestring step off the rope to safety. It occurred to me that there was nothing to stop me flying out of the arena and away over the rim of the mountain. A lesser bird would not have hesitated. Suddenly the thought was knocked out of my mind. The gloves came from nowhere.

*Oooofffff!* Stars exploded before my eyes and the world below began to spin like a roulette wheel.

A SIGH OF DISMAY ROSE FROM THE CROWD as Metropolis plummeted towards the ground.

'She's in a tailspin!' Violet grabbed her father's hand and gazed in horror.

'It's a nosedive,' Daisy said. She could hardly bear to look.

May's heart lurched as she watched through the telescope. Metropolis was spiralling towards her end.

'She's hit.' Daisy closed her eyes.

'No, she's not!' her sister cried, and when Daisy looked again the bird was climbing. The audience gasped with relief. Metropolis had raised her beak at the last moment. She was gaining height with every stroke of her wings.

'Metropolis!' Marm said the name through clenched teeth and it came out as a hiss. She turned to her guards. 'Get rid of that wretched bird!'

The guards took out slingshots and loaded them with the diamonds they carried in their back pockets for the purpose. *Twang! Twang! Twang!*

If Metropolis had time to think she would have marvelled at how the speed of her fall had powered her rise back into the sky, but her mind was fixed on the gloves. She was high above the pit and they were just above her. She was only dimly aware of the bright stones whizzing past. Each one missed. She was a moving target and she felt somehow invincible. She stopped flapping and let the momentum carry her towards her prey. Her mind slowed down. She focused on the seam of one of the gloves and her glide was silent and deadly.

She could see the individual stitches and when she stabbed, her aim was true.

Metropolis grabbed the thread and pulled it taut, twisting her head one way and the other in an attempt to reef it out. Her claws grasped the body of the glove and she tugged with all her might.

'Give me that, you fool!' Marm snatched the slingshot from the nearest guard and pulled a diamond from a string of precious stones that dangled from her left ear. She loaded the weapon and aimed. 'Damn! I missed!'

Marm quickly reloaded the slingshot. She took aim and fired again. Metropolis didn't mean to do a backflip but, when the thread came free, her head jerked over her heels and her tail followed.

Marm's stone would have made a direct hit but Metropolis was gone a split second before the

311

diamond arrived and the only bit of her it touched was the tip of her second tail feather. A cheer rose from the crowd.

'You'll pay for that!' Marm cried.

The macaw righted herself. She lowered her head and tucked the thread behind her spare claw, the fifth talon that was as sharp as her mind. Then she paused for a second, watching the glove come apart. Marm watched too. The pieces fell from the sky and floated past her into the pit. She stared in disbelief.

'That's right, Metropolis,' Sylvie yelled. 'Now get the other one!'

Metropolis's blood was up. She raised her crest and, with two powerful wingbeats, she was upon it. She must have grabbed the thread in just the right spot or perhaps the glove had been weakened by the loss of its partner, because the stitches came undone in one smooth movement. Metropolis held the thread in her beak. She scanned the throng, looking for Braid. The crowd roared. 'Bravo! Spectacular!'

Marm was furious. She watched the pieces of the second glove disappear into the pit. 'Well, don't just stand there, you fools,' she yelled to her guards. 'Go after them. Get them!'

The guards ran back along the walkway and around the rim of the mine until they reached the path that spiralled into its depths. Meanwhile, Metropolis swooped towards the audience. She spied Braid in the crowd and, although she was going too fast to stop, when Braid raised her hand to take the thread, Metropolis dropped it at exactly the right moment. Then she plummeted on and none of the troupe saw where she landed. Everyone was making their way towards Braid. She frayed one end of the thread, separating the fibres and then, squatting on the ground, she wound the other end onto the shaft of her spindle. She had to concentrate.

*Anticlockwise*, she thought. *Turn the whorl the wrong way.* She spun the whorl with her left hand and closed her eyes.

*'Tween Twixt and Twirl and kith and kin*
*Unsplit the light, unspin, unspin*
*The river winds by Warp on Twine*
*Unply the thread with hair so fine...'*

Sylvie held Daisy Ditto's hand and when Violet and Lobe arrived with the others, they all held hands and formed a little circle around Braid.

'That's it,' Sylvie said. '*Unply, unspin.*' She joined in and said the words with Braid and soon they were all chanting the rhyme. Braid spun the whorl faster and faster and everyone gasped when the thread divided into colour rays. Purple, indigo, blue, green, gold and crimson – all the colours of the rainbow streamed from the top of the spindle. They shot up into the air then arched above the crowd.

Shoestring had the best view. He was standing on the platform at the other side of the pit. From there he could see Marm on her stage. She held the Eye of the Dragon in one hand and she was gesturing into the hole with the other, while she shouted at her guards.

'Get the gloves! Get the pieces and bring them back immediately!'

She didn't see the coloured rays as they streamed towards the red diamond. There was a flash as they re-entered the stone and Marm, dazzled by the light, let out a scream and dropped her precious diamond into the pit.

'My darling!' she cried. 'Light of my life!'

She ran along the walkway to the edge of the mine and took the spiral path, racing downhill. The lights around the edge dimmed and the last thing Shoestring saw was Marm's silver hair streaming behind her as she disappeared into the darkness.

He looked up and scanned the crowd. Who was that tall man in the distance? Was it Lobe? And was that Ace standing beside him? Shoe might have been waking from a dream. He had a moment of sheer happiness when he recognised Lovegrove, Sylvie and KidGlovz. His friends! It was as if he hadn't seen them for years. But something was wrong; why were they all wearing black and why did Kid look so strange? Shoe's face clouded over as he remembered what he'd done, the things he'd taken when the gloves were on his hands. He looked beyond the crowd and saw the tower.

'May!' he cried.

Ace saw Shoestring pointing. 'Come on,' he yelled. 'May's in the tower.'

Shoestring climbed down the ladder and pushed his way through the crowds. He caught up with the troupe outside the House of Diamonds. There were no guards at the gate.

'This way,' he shouted, as he rushed through the main doors into the entrance hall.

'Look at that!' Daisy pointed to the ceiling. 'It's like a starry sky.'

'I saw it first,' said Violet.

Shoestring ran up the spiral staircase to the tower. The door was locked.

'Anyone got a pick?'

Violet took a butterfly clip from her hair. 'You can borrow it if you promise to give it back,' she said.

When Shoestring opened the door May ran to him and held him tight.

'You're safe,' she cried.

'For now.' Ace hugged them both. 'But the festival isn't over yet,' he said.

'Shoe, are you really all right?' May stepped back and looked at Shoestring carefully.

'I think so. I feel a bit dazed.'

'How do you think Kid feels?' Sylvie asked.

Shoestring turned to KidGlovz and looked at him closely. 'I'm so sorry, Kid,' he said. 'I really am.'

'What for?' Kid replied, puzzled. So much puzzled him lately.

'What's that smell?' Lobe asked, and out of habit Hugo sniffed the air. He gave a little whine and pressed against Lovegrove's leg. He couldn't smell a thing.

'Dad, look!' Daisy stared out the window. 'There's steam coming out of the ground.'

Violet held her nose. 'It smells like rotten eggs.'

'It's sulphur dioxide,' Sylvie told them. 'An odiferous vapour issuing from a deep fissure in the earth's crust. Volume XXVII page—'

'I think we should get away from here before that woman comes back,' Lovegrove said.

'Yes, let's go,' Shoestring agreed.

KidGlovz scratched his head. He was still pondering the last thing he'd heard.

'What are you sorry for?' he asked.

'He's sorry he took your mind away,' Sylvie said.

'Did he?'

Shoestring stared at his feet. 'Yes, Kid. I did,' he said. 'But maybe...' He closed his eyes and remembered the shadow on the tent wall. What did the goat-man say? *I'll take these stolen goods away ... I'll put them in the strongroom ...*

'But maybe I can get it back!' Shoe cried. He turned to May. 'Do you know where the strongroom is? Do you remember it?'

'How could I forget? It's in the basement below the entrance hall.'

May hurried away and everyone followed except Sylvie. She was gazing out the window.

'I'm speculating on the difference between an extinct volcano and a dormant one...' she muttered.

'Don't push, Daisy,' Violet said, as they made their way down the stairs.

'You're the one who's pushing,' her sister snapped.

May showed them a narrow staircase at the back corner of the entrance hall. It ended in a passageway that had a row of doors on either side. She looked away as she passed the maids' room where she used to sleep.

They reached a heavy wooden door. It was secured with a combination lock.

'This is it,' May said. 'The strongroom.'

Violet's hairclip snapped when Shoestring tried it in the lock. He needed something stronger.

'Use this,' May said, pulling a wire from the bustle of her dress. That broke as well.

Shoestring peered closely at the lock. He turned the little brass reels. There were six of them. 'How would you spell Jack in numbers?' he asked Sylvie.

She answered immediately: 'Ten, one, three, eleven.'

The lock sprang apart and Ace helped Shoestring push open the door.

preposter

potato dumplings

EVERYONE WAS BLOWN AGAINST THE WALLS by the force of the blast. Hugo gave a yelp and May heard a clunk as the telescope she was carrying hit the flagstones. She closed her eyes and waited for the dust to settle. When she opened them her cards were fluttering everywhere. Hugo was sniffing around and Lobe had his hands over his ears. KidGlovz seemed different. He was touching a little quaver earring that hung from his left ear. 'Where's my accordion?' he asked.

Lovegrove looked stunned. They all did. She sat against the door and blinked.

'It's with Mr Grimwade,' she replied.

'Mr Grimwade, I know him!' Kid helped Lovegrove to her feet and looked towards the twins.

'Dad, your ears have grown back,' the girls yelled in one voice.

Lobe stroked his long ears then cocked his head, listening. He did not look happy.

'What's wrong?' the twins asked. 'What is it?'

'I'm not sure. It might be just someone's stomach rumbling.' With a worried look Lobe put his ear to the ground.

# CHAPTER TWENTY-EIGHT

# THE EYE OF THE DRAGON

I WAS WOUNDED. OF COURSE I WAS. ALL GREAT heroes are wounded. I had bent one of my best wing feathers. There was nothing like a first aid tent at the Diamond Jubilee Festival of Marvels, and if it wasn't for the kindness of a small child who happened to notice me, I may well have been trampled underfoot. The festival, it seemed, had ended and people were in a hurry to leave.

'Poor birdie,' the child said. 'You were very brave.'

A boy squatted beside me, examining the damage.

'Broken?' he asked.

'Not the wing, but the feather,' I replied.

The child stared in surprise – but I was more surprised than he was. My voice had returned. I had spoken aloud!

The boy crouched closer to me and peered into my face as if he didn't believe what he'd heard. 'Hello, Cockie?' he asked, and was promptly rewarded with a sharp peck on the nose.

His eyes filled with tears and I saw he was very young, younger than Sylvie, and I knew I'd been a bit rough on him.

'Sorry, boy,' I said. 'But I've just defeated the enemy in a dangerous aerial battle and I can't abide being called *Cockie*.'

'I understand,' the boy whispered. He reached into his pocket, pulled out a handkerchief and wiped the blood from his nose.

I stared at the hanky. There was an insignia stitched in one corner, a picture of a fiddlehead fern.

MAY TRIED TO GATHER HER WITS. SHE WAS
shaken but she wasn't hurt. A couple of
cards lay face-down in her lap. She turned
one over.

'The Conflagration. What would
Metropolis say about that?' She looked
up.

'Where *is* Metropolis?' she cried.

'She was all right when I last saw her,'
Braid said. 'She won the battle.'

'Hear anything, Dad?' the Dittos asked.

Lobe got up from his hands and knees.
'The rumbling is coming from under the
ground. The mountain is restless.'

'We'd better get off it, then,' Sylvie
advised.

May scooped up her cards and tucked them into her dress.
She picked up the telescope. 'Let's go,' she cried.

The troupe ran along the passage and up the narrow stairs
to the entrance hall.

'How long have we got, Sylvie?' Lobe asked.

'It depends on the size of the vent, the internal temperature
and the pressure building beneath the earth's crust. We may
have weeks or maybe just minutes.'

'Look at that!' the Dittos cried as they ran through
the gates.

A crack opened in the ground in front of the twins and, holding hands, they leapt over it.

'It's red-hot down there,' they yelled.

Sylvie paused to stare. 'The points at which the vapours are copiously disgorged are called fumaroles,' she said, but nobody was listening. The troupe was running fast and so was the crowd up ahead.

Someone was shouting through a loudspeaker. 'Hurry! Everyone get off the mountain. It's going to erupt.' People

It's a superficial manifestation of forces deep beneath the earth's crust...

were already panicking, but this announcement caused a stampede.

May clung to Ace as she ran into the throng.

'Metropolis,' she cried. 'Where are you?' She could barely hear herself above the noise; people were shouting and screaming, their footsteps drummed the ground, and the mountain itself was making a low groaning sound.

Frantically May searched. 'We've got to find her.'

'There's no time,' Ace cried.

May put the telescope to her eye. The lens was shattered and the scene before her was a pattern of moving fragments.

She might have been looking through a kaleidoscope. When she pointed the lens back the way they'd come, the tower broke up into diamond-shaped shards.

Shoestring ran ahead, pushing his way through the crowd. He was heading for the scaffolding. When he reached the ladder he took the rungs two at a time. He untied his rope then ran to the far side of the pit. May followed, climbing up after him. She stood on the platform and scanned the crowd, but there was no sign of Metropolis.

'We have to go,' Shoe said, as he untied the other end of the rope then looped it over his shoulder.

He took the telescope and dropped it into the pit. Then, taking May's arm, he led her to the ladder and into the chaos below.

FRY THE POTATOES WITH THE ONIONS
*until golden brown … Chop up a handful of parsley and add sage and*
*wild thyme and sea salt …*

Grimwade leaned his exercise book against Haul as he wrote down the recipe. It was the potato dumpling dish his mother used to make.

A dull booming sound made him look up. A little white cloud hung over the top of the mountain like a puff of smoke. He could see people coming down the track.

'They're leaving in a hurry.' Grimwade frowned for a moment, then continued with his recipe. *Beat two eggs and add a handful of breadcrumbs …* It was all coming back to him now and he would get it down in writing in case he ever forgot it again.

Meanwhile, back on the mountain, people were yelling as they made their escape: 'Run. Run for your lives!'

KidGlovz held Hugo's collar and the dog howled in terror as he bounded forward. Tents were knocked over and people struggled to keep their footing in the rush.

'Stick together,' May cried. 'We don't want to lose each other.'

The boy held Metropolis tightly under his arm and she watched the world flash past. The air was full of dust and steam and things were being trampled underfoot: a macaw from the shooting gallery, the head of a laughing clown, some of the Cards of Life – The Abyss and The Tower. At one stage she saw the Legendary Flambé running past.

He'd lost his mask but she recognised his voice. 'I knew this would happen one day,' he cried.

She caught a glimpse of Braid up ahead, carrying her spindle and basket, but then Marm's henchmen blocked her view. They were running along with everyone else. The Wheel of Fortune lay on the ground, spinning wildly.

'I'M COMING, MY SHINING ONE,' MARM cried, as she ran down the narrow pathway into the mine.

The pit was not bottomless as some people thought; the path spiralled twenty-five times before it reached the floor, and although the lights had gone out Marm knew exactly where she was – she had designed the mine herself. She had watched it being dug and supervised the construction of the tunnels that led out from the base. There were thirteen of them, and each one ended in a shaft. She also knew there were two winds that blew within the mine – the updraft and the downdraft. She hoped the downdraft had sucked the pieces of the gloves into one of the tunnels and that her guards had followed them. She couldn't trust the guards with the Eye of the Dragon. Any one of them could pick it up; even the most loyal of her men would not resist temptation if they saw the stone glowing in the dark.

She ran faster. 'I'm coming, my precious,' she called.

The diamond was bright in her mind, so bright it seemed to give off heat as well as light. There was a slight smell of burning and if Marm's cheeks grew red and the hairs in her nostrils felt singed, she barely noticed, for she was a woman whose mind was on fire. If she heard a low rumbling sound, she put it down to her own inner quakings, her fear of losing what she loved most.

By the time she reached the twenty-first circle of the path, smoke burned her throat and tears stung her eyes. She paused and leaned on the rock wall, which was as hot as she was.

The diamond would not be difficult to find, she thought. It would have landed directly below the platform on which she'd been standing and it would be waiting there, shining for her. She looked down into the blackness, surprised she couldn't see it already.

The base of the pit was smaller than the top. It was a hundred paces across. Marm knew because she had decided on the measurements. It was not a large area to search. All she needed to do was call and the Eye of the Dragon would light her way.

'How wise you are, my darling,' she breathed. 'Hiding your light until I arrive.'

She continued down the path and when she reached the twenty-third circle, the smoke and steam was so thick she realised the task of finding her treasure was not going to be as easy as she thought. What to do? She took a deep breath and at that moment the mountain did too; a downdraft cleared the smoke from the bottom of the pit and drew it into the tunnels.

What luck! she thought. There was her jewel, exactly where she'd expect it to be!

The diamond glowed like a hot coal, and when Marm called, it brightened with a fiery light that threw flickering shadows onto the rock wall. The stone was only a dozen or so steps from the end of the path. Marm raced to the bottom. She couldn't wait to reach her prize. The floor of the pit was red-hot and burned the soles off her shoes, but she didn't care. It was a small price to pay for recovering her treasure.

'My darling one, my brightest star,' she cried, as she reached for the diamond.

A second later Mount Adamantine erupted.

# STAR

## PART SEVEN

# CHAPTER TWENTY-NINE

# THE RISING STAR

HUGO DIDN'T NOTICE KIDGLOVZ SNIPPING off the tufts of long hair that grew down the back of his legs, and if he had noticed he wouldn't have minded. He was gazing at Grimwade's cooking pot and his nostrils quivered. It was wonderful to smell again. He wagged his tail and barked with excitement.

Braid spun the dog hair carefully, turning the whorl clockwise, the old way, and breathing deeply as the thread twisted between her fingers. The strands were long and wiry and the thread seemed strong, but she wouldn't be sure until she'd made enough to test it. She didn't need a lot; an arm's length would be plenty, she thought as she wound the thread onto the spindle and took the handful of hair KidGlovz was offering.

'The best hair is on his tail,' KidGlovz said. 'But he won't keep still. Do you need more?'

Braid nodded. She actually had enough dog hair but it was so good to be spinning again that she didn't want to stop. She teased out the long fibres, and as they spun through her fingers she allowed herself to imagine the future like a long unbroken thread. She closed her eyes and in her mind she saw Peg, Fray and Twill sitting at their looms weaving again, making marvellous cloth.

'I hope everyone likes potato dumplings,' Grimwade called from the camp kitchen. Mrs Silverstrings replied that her family loved potato dumplings; they had first tried them when they were on tour near Lake Ostinato.

Her twelve children were gathered around her, and Sylvie was among them. Mrs Silverstrings held the little girl's hand and tried to hide her tears. 'Your name's not Sylvie Quickfingers,' she said. 'It's Sylvie Silverstrings. We've missed you so much.'

'But I don't remember you.' Sylvie stared into the woman's green eyes. There was something familiar about them though. With a start she realised they were like her own eyes.

'You were very young when we lost you,' the woman said. 'You were only two. You went missing after a performance. We searched everywhere and when we couldn't find you, we lost heart.'

'We thought you'd fallen off a cliff and died,' the youngest Silverstrings boy shouted enthusiastically.

'Glen, be quiet. You weren't even born then.'

Mr Silverstrings saw that Sylvie was feeling overwhelmed.

'Everyone, go and play,' he said. 'Give the girl some breathing space.'

His wife waited until most of the children had run off before she continued. 'We searched high and low. We thought we'd lost you forever.'

Sylvie didn't know what to think. She looked to Lovegrove.

'Sylvie wasn't lost,' Lovegrove told Mrs Silverstrings. 'She was stolen.' She opened the Dittos' book and pointed to the picture of her brother, Eronius Spin.

'He stole musical children,' she explained. 'He stole KidGlovz. When he went away I inherited the house and the children.'

'Lovegrove adopted me.' Suddenly tears welled in Sylvie's eyes.

'Don't be sad, Sylvie. Be happy,' Lovegrove said. 'Now you've got two mothers.'

Myrtle, the youngest daughter, put her hand on Sylvie's knee. 'Fiddleback Mountain is beautiful, Sylvie. I'll show it to you.'

'And I'll show you Cadenza Towers.' Sylvie smiled through her tears.

'SQUAWK! SQUAWK!'

I had resolved to keep a low profile during the reunion between Sylvie and her family — meeting your mother after all those years must be a delicate thing — but Shoestring had given me back my mirror and as I gazed into its depths I realised a low profile didn't suit me at all. I lifted my head, raised my fabulous crest and let out a series of ear-splitting cries to bring everyone to attention. I felt it was time for a formal announcement. I wanted to tell people that a certain member of the troupe had distinguished herself in action and was about to be presented with an award. I had prepared the acceptance speech in my head. It irked me that I had to present the award as well as accept it, but if I didn't do it, who would? Everyone was so busy they didn't notice the marvellous macaw in their midst.

A double bass was leaning against the wagon behind Sylvie. I landed on its scroll and cleared my throat.

'The Fabulous Macaw is known not only for the brilliance of her plumage but for the brilliance of her mind.' I paused for effect and was disappointed to see that May was the only one listening to me.

'Metropolis, it was so quiet when you didn't have a voice,' she sighed.

Nobody else was taking any notice. Mrs Silverstrings was talking to Lovegrove.

'Sylvie could read when she was still a baby,' she said, 'and by the time she was two she could play all our songs with variations.'

Mr Silverstrings had produced a photo album and was showing Sylvie pictures of herself when she was an infant.

'Look, it's my violin!' Sylvie exclaimed.

'I made it for you when you were born, Sylvie,' he said. 'I make all the family's instruments.'

It was outrageous to be ignored like this — not only was I responsible for bringing Sylvie back to the flock, I had risked life and limb to save Shoestring's life. I slid my beak down one of the strings of the double bass and made a long, whining sound, then I gave the string a good hard pluck. It broke with a twang and Mr Silverstrings looked up. 'Oh dear,' he remarked vaguely. 'And I haven't got any spares.' Then he went on talking to Sylvie as if nothing had happened.

Sylvie was enjoying herself now. She had one arm around Lovegrove and the other around her new little sister, Myrtle. Her mother and father were kneeling at her feet pointing at the album.

I flew off in a huff and landed on the bough of a tree near Shoestring and his companions.

'You can feel it but you can't see it,' he was telling them. Ten pairs of green eyes gazed in wonder at Shoestring's invisible rope.

'Can you teach us?' the oldest Silverstrings boy asked. 'We're good at heights. We're always climbing trees back home.'

'We'll start low.' Shoestring tied the rope a short distance off the ground. 'Who wants to try?'

'Let Laurel go first.' The boy pointed to his sister.

A little girl in a dress the colour of moss took Shoestring's hand and stepped onto the rope. 'We can all learn,' she said. 'We can walk the rope and play fiddle at the same time.'

'Excuse me,' I shrieked. 'Everyone has to attend a meeting at the wagon immediately.'

'No, Metropolis. We're busy.' It was the boy who had rescued me. 'Shoestring's showing us the ropes.'

'It's an emergency meeting!'

'All right. In a minute,' Shoestring muttered, and there were grumbles all round.

'Is she always this bossy?' the little boy asked.

'Always,' Shoestring replied as I flew away.

I landed on Daisy Ditto's shoulder. She and Violet and some of the girls were playing near the wagon.

'Quiet, Metropolis,' she said, before I had a chance to speak. 'Don't make them lose their balance.'

'These girls are supple as vines,' Violet remarked. 'They're doing the grasshopper.'

'We could never do it properly because we didn't have enough legs,' Daisy laughed. 'Their names are Fern, Tansy and Ivy.'

'I don't care what their names are,' I said. 'Everyone has to come to a meeting. It's starting right now.'

'All right,' Daisy sighed. 'But first things first — we need to show them the butterfly.'

*First things first?* Surely Metropolis should come first! It was exasperating — more than exasperating — it was unforgivable! I flew over to Braid and landed next to her basket. As you know I don't have a high opinion of pigeons but I needed an audience, someone who would sit still and listen, and the bird was trapped.

'Sylvie and the Silverstrings would never have found each other if it wasn't for me,' I muttered and, to its credit, the bird responded with sympathetic cooing sounds. Braid took no notice. She was writing a note.

'Can you read, Metropolis?' she asked.

'Of course.' I read the note aloud. '"Dear Peg, Fray and Twill, All is well. I'll be home soon, love Braid."'

She folded the note small. 'Now for the test,' she said.

I watched Braid wind a short length of thread around her finger and pull it taut.

'It holds, Metropolis,' she breathed. 'I can spin again!'

She took the pigeon from the basket and tied the note around its leg. Then she kissed the bird gently on the head and let it go.

We watched it fly between the two wagons as it headed out over the lake. Then, to my surprise, Braid turned and kissed me on the head as well.

'Thank you, Metropolis,' she said. 'It's all due to you.'

I felt my spirit rise. It was like the wind under my wings.

'Thank you for getting the thread and thank you for saving your friends, Shoestring and KidGlovz. You'll always be welcome in Loom and Spindle Reach. I hope you'll visit one day.'

'It was nothing really,' I mumbled. 'I'm just a humble fowl of the air.'

'No, Metropolis.' Braid looked into my eyes. 'You were truly marvellous.'

She was about to go on, but Grimwade called everyone for dinner.

AFTER THE MEAL, BRAID SAID IT WAS TIME for her to go home. 'But before I do, I wish to make a presentation,' she said. 'This little basket may not seem much, but it was made by my great-grandmother from twigs of the silverwood trees that grow in the Twixt. It's fine and strong and it will last forever. Please accept it as a gift, Metropolis. Think of it as the Fame and Fortune Award for Courage in the Face of Adversity.'

Everyone cheered so loudly that my acceptance speech flew out of my head and by the time Braid had said her goodbyes, it still hadn't returned.

May decided we should leave as well. She was keen to get

back to the Luck Palace. Ruby, Mr Goldfiend and the others would be wondering what had happened to her.

'We'll go first thing tomorrow,' she said. 'Shoestring, will you come with us?'

Shoestring wasn't listening. He had cut off a length of his rope and was using a strand of it to fix Sylvie's grandfather's double bass.

'Will it stay in tune, son?' the old man asked.

'Let's see.'

One of Sylvie's brothers helped Shoe tighten the string. Then he tested it.

'It's good. Let's replace the other strings as well.'

'People won't believe it.' The man shook his head. 'Music from invisible strings!'

Sylvie held up her violin. 'Do mine,' she cried.

Soon all the Silverstrings' instruments were lined up in front of Shoestring.

'I'll write some new music,' KidGlovz decided. 'Songs for accordion and —' he counted '— forty-eight invisible strings.'

It was then that I had one of those exceptionally good ideas for which the Fabulous Macaw is renowned.

'You can call yourselves The Invisible String Band!' I declared. 'You can join forces with the Troupe of Marvels and tour together.'

The old man, Pop Silver, was so excited by this thought that he grabbed the nearest fiddle and played a tune.

Mrs Silverstrings smiled. 'Our family has suddenly grown,' she said.

'And so has our troupe,' Shoestring added proudly.

'You'll travel to Goat Mountain,' I told them. 'There's a big crowd waiting to be entertained.'

MAY LIKED THE IDEA OF EVERYONE travelling together and so did Lovegrove, although both of them had decided to go back to Cadenza.

'I'll throw a spread for the boys,' May said. 'Just to be sure.'

Half the pack of May's cards had been lost along the way, so maybe the odds were stacked in the boys' favour. She drew The Rising Star and it was the right way up.

Shoestring looked back at Mt Adamantine. Already it seemed far away. He thought of himself running up there on the night he first left the troupe, the gloves lighting his way. He saw himself racing past the queue on his way to the festival, desperate to get to the top in time for the competition. He gazed at his hands, which were his own now, the hands of an ordinary boy. Then he looked at May and his friends, who were anything but ordinary, and thought how lucky he was. Even Metropolis, who had landed on his shoulder so as not to miss out on anything, didn't annoy him. His feet were planted firmly on the ground and his heart was so light he might have been walking on air.

SUPPORTED BY

Tasmanian
Government

This project was assisted through Arts Tasmania
by the Minister for the Arts

First published by Allen & Unwin in 2020

Allen & Unwin
83 Alexander Street
Crows Nest NSW 2065
Australia
Phone: (61 2) 8425 0100
Email: info@allenandunwin.com
Web: www.allenandunwin.com

 A catalogue record for this
book is available from the
National Library of Australia

ISBN 978 1 76029 721 3

For teaching resources, explore www.allenandunwin.com/resources/for-teachers

Cover design by Joanna Hunt
Cover illustration by Dale Newman
Text design by Ruth Grüner and Joanna Hunt
Set in 12.2 pt Bembo by Joanna Hunt
Illustrations in oil-based charcoal pencil and watercolour wash on paper

Printed in February 2020 by C&C Offset Printing Co. Ltd, China

10 9 8 7 6 5 4 3 2 1

## ACKNOWLEDGEMENTS

I am grateful to Varuna, the Writer's House, for the Eleanor Dark Flagship Fellowship, during which I wrote the first chapters and for the generous support from the May Gibbs Children's Literature Trust whose Creative Time Fellowship helped me complete the final draft.

Special thanks to Erica Wagner for the inspired conversations and to Sue Flockhart for guiding the way with ease and humour as the book found its form. Thanks also to designers Ruth Grüner and Jo Hunt who brought the words and images together so successfully, and to Kate Whitfield whose excellent editing shaped the story.

And thanks always to Dale Newman for her wonderful drawings, the laughter and the great collaboration. JULIE

Eternal, heartfelt thanks to Erica Wagner and Sue Flockhart for their generous guidance and encouragement from the beginning, to Julie Hunt for her inspired stories and friendship, to Kate Whitfield, Ruth Grüner and Jo Hunt for their individual and collective brilliance, and to my angels – Ali and Raf – for their love, support and patience. DALE

# ABOUT THE AUTHOR

Julie Hunt loves storytelling and traditional folktales. Her stories combine other-worldly elements with down-to-earth humour. She loves travel and is fascinated by landscapes and the tales they inspire. This interest has taken her from the rugged west coast of Ireland to the ice caves of Romania where she collected ideas for her graphic novel, *KidGlovz*, illustrated by Dale Newman. *KidGlovz* won the 2016 Queensland Literary Award and her latest novel, *Shine Mountain*, was shortlisted for the 2019 NSW Premier's Award. She has received many awards and commendations for earlier books, including winning Readings' inaugural Children's Book Prize for *Song for a Scarlet Runner* in 2014 and the Children's Book Council of Australia Picture Book of the Year Award for *The Coat*, illustrated by Ron Brooks, in 2013.

# ABOUT THE ILLUSTRATOR

Dale Newman creates images full of mystery, high drama and subtle humour, so her collaboration with Julie Hunt on *KidGlovz* and *Shoestring, the Boy Who Walks on Air* has been a natural fit. She has a background in lithography and etching, which brings a love of rendering light and tone to her pencil illustrations. Her distinctive work has appeared on gallery walls, newspapers, magazines and educational books for children. She has also worked extensively as an artist in the youth health sector, and uses these skills in workshops she runs with Julie in schools around Australia.

Dale lives with her partner and son and their talkative dog on the NSW south coast. In her spare time she can be found rescuing dilapidated retro chairs from the jaws of the council crunchy truck.

# GO BACK TO THE BEGINNING...

'Mysterious, fantastic and gripping.' *Good Reading*

'Stunning...to be remembered for a long time.' BookTrust (UK)

WINNER : Queensland Literary Awards,
Griffith University Children's Book Award

SHORT-LISTED : CBCA Book of the Year,
Crichton Award for New Illustrators